Westbourne

Westbourne

STEPHEN TOURISH

ISBN-13: 9781530612765
ISBN-10: 1530612764

Table of Contents

Chapter 1

No One Ever Pays Much Attention To The Guy In The Front

Thursday the 13th December 2012. 12.45pm on a very cold, crisp winter's afternoon. The temperature of London was finally starting to rise ever so slightly after last night's freezing fog. Last night had seen a low of minus four degrees Celsius in London and it was still only one degree Celsius now.

Tammar is parked in his black London taxi cab at the head of the rank in Seville Street in-between the Harvey Nichols department store and the Park Tower hotel and casino in Knightsbridge. He's partway through his working day as a London black taxi driver. He quite likes this time of year despite traffic being heavier in central London and journey times slower. The Christmas decorations are up around town and his two children are counting down the number of 'sleeps' til Christmas. He likes the variety of passengers in one day this time of year brings too. Everyone is still in work. Kids are still at school. People are out Christmas shopping. The evening crowds go out to the theatre and the office parties come later. If he's pulling a sixteen-hour day in the run up to Christmas he will probably try to catch a job in 'going home mode' at the end of the night, where for 70% of the meter you take the London Underground staff home.

Once the London Underground shuts down, black taxis on a radio circuit follow the different tube lines out of London taking the night staff home.

A few hours later you then get the same thing in reverse as the black cabs bring the morning staff back into town following the tube lines back in. So, depending on the length of his day and whether he decides to do earlies, lates or nights it will be a very busy and mixed crowd today.

A pedestrian has been struck by a motorcycle and then run over by a double decker bus at nearby Hyde Park corner and traffic in this part of town has become very, very slow. He is relishing a ten-minute break from driving and a chance to get out of the cab to perform a few stretches and a quick flick through the Sun newspaper.

He is dressed in a smart casual, thin grey jumper, white t-shirt, dark blue jeans, scarf and a dark cheese cutter flat cap.

Despite being 40 years old, he has taken this opportunity while waiting for his next fare to get out and stretch his legs and lower back next to the cab as he has previously slipped a disc in his back twice and suffers from occasional back pain and sciatica. He doesn't want to leave the warmth of the cab but he knows that if he doesn't put his coat on and get out and stretch a bit now he'll regret it later.

As he's at the head of the rank, he's first in line for whoever should need a cab and so after a few stretches he's happy to take his coat back off and get back into the warmth of the cab and out of the very cold December afternoon.

He puts the Sun newspaper on the steering wheel and mutters to himself, "Gangnam Style Dance Kills Dad" as he reads the front-page headline and immediately turns past it. He starts to flick through the newspaper until finally he catches a story that he thinks is worthy of reading. He becomes so engrossed in the article he's a little embarrassed that he hasn't noticed a gentleman approach from his left-hand side, open the rear passenger door and start to get in. Tammar clicks on the intercom and a small red bulb illuminates inside a switch next to the passenger.

"Where would you like to go sir?"

He doesn't particularly trust the public and believes that by calling someone sir it momentarily mentally unbalances them and puts them on his side. He is also pleased that it shows his willingness to serve and a good attitude to customer service. After all, these are the people who pay his wages and put food on the table to support his family as he is the sole bread earner.

"High Road Chigwell."

A nice long run outside of London. His luck is in. Tammar lives in the village next to Chigwell, Abridge. He'll be able to pop in and say a quick hello to his long-term partner, Christine, and have a cup of green tea.

"Yes sir." He clicks the intercom off. Folding the newspaper once, he throws it onto the floor beside him and starts the meter.

He turns the ignition key and the diesel engine roars to life. As he does this the passenger is saying something. He doesn't quite catch it.

The switch next to the passenger in the back of the cab glows red to indicate that Tammar has switched the intercom on once more.

He looks into his rear view mirror at the smartly dressed white male who looks to be about the same forty years old as Tammar.

"I'm sorry sir, I missed that?"

"I said can you avoid Hyde Park Corner, it's chock-a-block. Any idea what's happened?"

"An old lady has been hit by a motorcycle and then run over by a double decker bus. Nasty business. It's been very busy round there with crowds going to the Winter Wonderland funfair and market. All being well I hope to take the missus and kids up there ice skating at the…" Pfff. A pop over the intercom means that the passenger has turned the intercom off from his side of the partition mid conversation. Tammar looks back in his rear view mirror at the passenger who is completely ignoring him and looking out the side window whilst reaching into his pocket for his mobile phone.

'Not a talker then' Tammar thinks to himself.

Because of the congestion around the Hyde Park Corner area Tammar is forced to avoid the area completely. From Seville Street he drives down Lowndes Square, Lowndes Street, Chesham Street, and Eaton Terrace. As they come out at Cliveden Place, he intends to turn left and head down towards Victoria station but that still looks heavily congested too. He chooses to go straight down into Eaton Terrace and makes his way to the Grosvenor Road where he can resume his intended route out of town along the Thames.

The passenger is absorbed in his telephone call in the back of the cab. From time to time he glances at Tammar's eyes in the rear view mirror. This is pretty much all he can see of him. There is the video screen in the back of the cab directly behind Tammar's head. His flat cap conceals the top of his head. So all that can be seen from behind is his eyes in the rear view mirror, not that the passenger is really paying that much attention to him. He speaks far too freely into his mobile phone assuming that the partition between them and the engine noise is enough to keep his conversation from being overheard. How wrong he is. Depending on the ebb and flow of the engine noise Tammar is only able to catch snippets of the passenger's conversation…

"…currently about five mill in the shop…and that's trade value, not retail…tonight…flying out…Mzungu they call me. Hey, like I give a damn. I fly over there. I give them U.S. dollars they give me the stones. Yeah! I go over the odds, about $20 for a loose stone they've found. They think they've made it when I put hard currency in their hands especially as I'm known for paying over the going rate. I sneak them back into the country by the handful, have them polished up no questions asked in Hatton Garden, and retail that $20 stone in Knightsbridge for £1,500. It's a licence to print money!

…Sure! …Kimberley Process Certified… I bring back some 'legit' ones in brick shaped packages to give my trip a reason for tax and authority purposes but the real deal for me is in the smuggling … You get the right certificates then you're good to bring them back in the country…$150… They're all so corrupt over there… Poor like you've never seen. You wave hard currency under their nose and they will stamp your certificates for you no problem… Security? I pay the police. They'll collect me from the airport, act as my body-guard and keep me and my stones safe until I'm back on the plane. I'm the goose laying the golden eggs for them.

I'm involved in a sixty plus billion dollar a year industry… The joke is these things aren't even rare or precious. It's all brilliantly clever marketing. Buy my love! They've managed to closely associate love with these naturally occurring plentiful stones. Basically you have to 'buy' your woman's love don't you with these plentiful stones? You hoard them. Control the supply. They appear rare. They're not!

Basically it's underground volcanoes creating and pushing up these stones to the surface. Da Beers were the farmers who sold their farm and that's where you get the phrase 'acres of diamonds' ".

Tammar can't believe his ears. This ranks up there with some of the most interesting and famous people he's had and conversations of regular folks he's ever overheard whilst driving the cab. The passenger doesn't realise that he's being overheard. As he continues, the conversation takes a chilling turn.

"Yeah, did another one the other night, it's on the news at the moment. Go on the BBC website. Some blonde, Essex bird slag. Slipped her a Rohypnol, she won't remember much, not enough to identify me."

Tammar becomes especially observant of the conversation now because he knows a young blonde lady who has just been the victim of rape where a date rape drug was used and she lives in Essex.

He is disgusted by what he is hearing and starts to feel very uneasy. His mind races…What should he do? Does he pull over and get the authorities? What if he is actually talking about Karen and it turns out that he attacked Karen? What are the odds of there being two Essex rapists in the last few days that used a date rape drug?

Karen's grandfather, Alfie, is a very old friend of Tammar and lives in the same village. He is a real old school East End villain. Tammar first met Alfie nearly thirty years ago when Tammar was working on the family market stall in the East End of London in Brick Lane in the Sunday market. Alfie was introduced as 'a man with access to guns'.

Grandad Alfie was amongst other things a commercial property burglar and armed robber - a blagger. Back then Alfie had a young granddaughter, Annie, who was very ill and in need of expensive operations. Tammar clearly remembers Alfie saying,

"There's not a sub post office round here that's safe until I get the money she needs for her operations."

Tammar held a quiet respect for Alfie from that time. Whilst yes, it was very wrong what he was doing, there was also a certain Robin Hood nobility to it. He wondered to himself what he would be prepared to do if there was a glimmer of hope for someone he loved.

The conversation from the passenger continues. It's starting to sound like Karen may well be who he is talking about and is not his first victim but rather that there have been tens of victims similar to Andrew Luster, the serial rapist and heir to the Max Factor cosmetics fortune who got tracked down by Dog the Bounty Hunter to Mexico. The modus operandi on each occasion is sounding the same. Slip the girls Rohypnol in their drinks so they can't remember anything about him and then rape them a little later on into the night.

Tammar thinks quickly. He could pull over and call the cops on him but listening to him with his Rohypnol he doesn't know if the authorities could secure a conviction, if Karen could necessarily remember enough; he'd be bound to claim consensual and at the most he'd get done for just the attack on Karen.

No, far better that Tammar keeps on listening and lets him keep on digging a hole like you wouldn't believe.

Tammar thinks to himself…

"You're going to be bang in trouble my friend. Bang in trouble."

As they stop at the traffic lights by the Tower of London, Tammar looks out at the Christmas decorations but his attention is snapped back as the passenger pulls a cigarette out of a packet, puts it to his lips and lights it despite there being a number of no smoking stickers.

He clicks on the intercom:

"Excuse me sir, I'm sorry but you can't smoke in the back of the cab it's against the law."

"Why don't you just be quiet and drive your cab for your bit of corn. I'll smoke if I like."

Tammar can't believe his ears! Usually at this point the passenger would be told in no uncertain terms to put the cigarette out. But he thinks to himself to bite on his tongue. The beginnings of a plan are starting to form in his mind.

The traffic lights change and the taxi drives on once more as the passenger puffs away arrogantly on his cigarette in the back of the cab.

'Don't show your hand Tam, don't show your hand', he thinks to himself. He mustn't give the game away and let the passenger know that anything is up. He must keep his poker face and not show the hand of cards he is holding.

The meter goes higher and higher as they exit the built up areas of the City of London and the office blocks as they go along the Whitechapel Road and the A12.

Before the journey is over the passenger has smoked a second cigarette which Tammar said nothing about and both cigarette stubs are left on the floor of the cab.

As they near their destination Tammar knows he wants to get a little more information out of him so he clicks on the intercom and tries to start up a conversation once again.

"Nice area this part of Chigwell. Do you live out here?"

"Yes, you'll see it in a couple of minutes. Detached, 6 bed, 5 bath, swimming pool, triple heated garage, grounds. Mortgage free."

'Mortgage free!' Anyone else would be satisfied with the rest of it. He just had to put in the mortgage free bit didn't he? Slime ball!' Tammar thinks!

"Do you have to travel much in your line of work?"

"Yes, I've got to fly out tonight actually."

"Oh really? Stanstead?"

"No. Heathrow."

"Would you like me to pick you up later sir and drive you out there? They are predicting freezing fog again and a low of minus five degrees Celsius tonight." Another tasty job. Tammar hopes that the passenger will go for it as he's starting to hatch a little plan.

"Can do driver. Six o'clock at mine. Ring the buzzer at the gate."

"Will do sir. I'll bring a couple of magazines for you to read on the journey."

"That's not necessary."

"They're the two latest copies of the Robb Report magazine. I think you might like them."

"Oh! The Robb Report! Oh yes! Bring those would you!"

The Robb Report is an American magazine not in general circulation in England and is hard to buy unless, like Tammar, you have a subscription to it. It shows the best of the best in the world. The best watches, the best cars, the best cigars, etc.

As they reach their destination on the High Road of Chigwell they pass a row of six-foot tall privacy fences before coming to a black double entrance gate. The passenger pulls a small remote control from the inside pocket of his Barbour quilted jacket and the two gates automatically open inwards.

Tammar drives past the gates which start to close behind them, and up a long drive which curves to the left dotted with trees before you come to a fountain surrounded by little box hedging in front of the house with a triple garage to the left.

A stunningly beautiful, sprawling mansion of a property in an incredible setting. It probably goes back a fair way too although Tammar can only see the front of the house.

It doesn't seem fair. Tammar is not a jealous or envious man in the slightest. If someone else has got it then good luck to them. He knows he could have it too if he put his mind to it but he does think to himself that he drives a cab for over fifty hours a week, sometimes working a sixteen-hour day to scrape by making an honest living and here is a serial rapist, diamond smuggler living in the lap of luxury.

If he was a good person and earned his living honestly then good luck to him but after what Tammar has been listening to during their journey out here it doesn't seem right.

The cherry on top of the injustice of life, is the passenger's three month old, beautiful dark granite grey coloured Maserati GranTurismo Sport parked next to a silver Audi TT. His wife comes to the front door to greet them.

In a very proud voice the passenger says, "There is my beauty (referring to the Maserati) and my fat cow of a miserable wife! Fat ugly bitch!"

Framed in the doorway is a good looking, 5 foot 4 inch tall blonde, wearing a baby blue velour tracksuit and tan Ugg Boots in her early to mid thirties.

"Look at her eh!? You can take the girl out of Essex but you can't take the Essex out of the girl. She lives in a £4 million pound house and dresses like a fucking chav!"

The passenger's wife is far from fat or ugly. Tammar thinks she may be carrying a couple of extra pounds but his snapshot of the situation is that she is unloved and neglected and looks far, far from happy.

Tammar tries to keep his face and chin down and out of sight as he tells the passenger the fare is £64.60 and thanks him for the 40p tip.

You get the feeling the £64.60 on the meter doesn't seem to faze the passenger at all as he hands over £65 in cash.

He may only tip 40 pence but you get the impression it's all small change to him. The expensive run out here and the prospect of an expensive run out to Heathrow later that night doesn't seem to bother him at all.

After an exchange of unpleasantries with his wife on the doorstep the passenger goes into the house. She rolls her eyes at Tammar as if to say 'I wish he'd drop down dead'. Tammar guesses that she is far from happy in her marriage and might have let herself go a bit for one reason or another.

Before departing, he makes a quick note of the registration plates of the two cars parked outside the house on a taxi receipt before driving back down towards the black automatic gates which start to open as the cab approaches.

Despite it being less than 3 miles back to Tammar's house he pulls over to the side of the road at the first safe spot to do so.

He gets out of the cab and goes to the boot and gets out a pair of latex gloves from next to his tool kit and a new, small, Ziploc brand, zip up bag and a pair of tweezers.

Tammar looks at us, the reader, and looks at the tweezers and says, "Don't ask."

He puts on the latex gloves and goes into the back of the cab and using the tweezers picks up the first of the two cigarette butts and puts it carefully in the Ziploc bag

"Now, let me get you before Mr Jug cross contaminates you. Oh yes, I know just who to speak to about you my serial rapist friend."

He puts the second of the cigarette butts in the bag and seals it up.

"It is a small world after all."

Chapter 2
Knowledge And Hidden Rivers

After using the tweezers to put the passenger's two cigarette butts into the Ziploc bag, Tammar resumes the drive home to Abridge. We see his eyes in the rear view mirror once more and he speaks to us once again.

"Now, I've held quite a few jobs in my time before doing The Knowledge. For those of you that don't know, The Knowledge is what all London black cab drivers must learn and pass before being given their badge and being allowed to work. It took me a little over three and a half years. It's like mental Sat Nav or GPS. The part of the brain for memory and navigation, the hippocampus, actually grows. It's amazing what you pick up. Of course once you pass out you don't stop learning. As they say, "you learn something everyday". For instance, did you know that 250 years ago London was no bigger than today's zone 1? The surrounding areas had a number of rivers running through them, at least 19 of them. As the city grew the central ones became covered over, a bit like sewers although not necessarily so.

Take our jeweller/rapist friend earlier. He may not realise it himself but his shop sits over the river Westbourne. The river starts in Hampstead and goes underground. It rises and makes a little water feature in Hyde Park called 'the Dell' at the end of the Serpentine lake, before going back under 'Rotten Row', South Carriage Drive, and exiting the park at Albert Gate in-between the embassies of Kuwait and France.

River Westbourne at The Dell - Hyde Park, London

River Westbourne flows under here to exit Hyde Park at Albert Gate.

Albert Gate. Kuwait embassy on the left of picture
and the French embassy on the right.

It goes underneath the A4 Knightsbridge road and flows right alongside the basement of matey's shop in William Street.

His shop is on the corner of William Street and Knightsbridge and has a postal address of 93 Knightsbridge, SW1.

I was on the point of the rank at Seville Street which is a stone's throw from his shop, Cloacina jewellers. He knows he can always get a cab from there no problem at all. There was gridlock at Hyde Park Corner, Grosvenor Place and Belgrave Square because of the bus running that old woman over. So we pretty much followed the route of the river Westbourne to avoid the area. From the rank at Seville Street, leave on the left, south down Lowndes Square, Lowndes Street, Chesham Street to Eaton Terrace near Sloane Square then we start to separate from it as it makes its way to the Thames.

By the time the river reaches Sloane Square station it can be seen in a big pipe flowing above the two platforms and tracks.

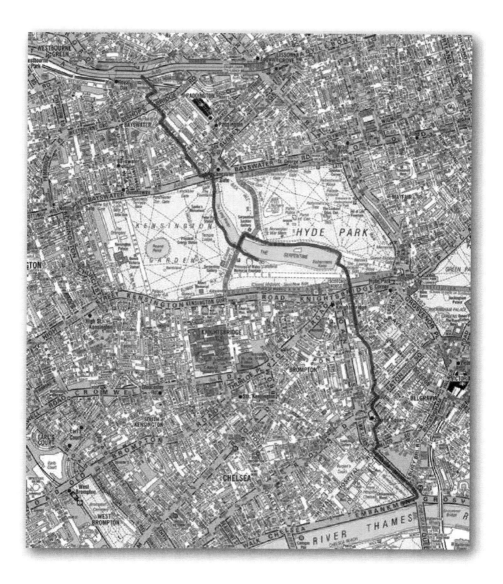

   In fact, did you know that's the only place on the entire London Underground network where a river is above the track? Everywhere else they managed to get it underneath the track but they couldn't manage it there. It's funny what you pick up isn't it? Anyway, the river flows above the tracks at Sloane Square station then continues down Holbein Place, Chelsea Bridge Road and then under Ranelagh Gardens before coming out into the Thames by Chelsea Bridge.

River Westbourne seen in green above platforms and tracks,
flowing from right to left over Sloane Square station

River Westbourne exit into the Thames

Amongst the jobs I've held in my time between leaving school and eventually doing The Knowledge, I've worked down the markets, under the railway arches in Bermondsey, I've worked for the Home Office and signed the Official Secrets Act. Eventually I got a job in a call centre for a black cab firm and that's where I decided to do The Knowledge.

What's all this got to do with our story I hear you ask? Well, good point. This brings us to our first port of call. But first let's park up the cab and go and see a man about a dog."

Eleven minutes later Tammar pulls up on the tarmac drive outside his three bedroom semi detached house on London Road, Abridge, Essex opposite the Shell petrol station. It's covered in Christmas lights and decorations and at the side of the house is an 8 year old, blue Ford Focus car. From inside the house he can hear excited barks from a little dog who he knows recognises the sound of the engine from the cab and will be watching him out of the sitting room bay window. He takes his coin dispenser and Ziploc bag with the passenger's two cigarette butts in and lets himself in the front door.

A longhaired Dachshund excitedly greets Tammar as soon as he crosses the threshold.

"Hello Toby me old china! Where's mummy? Go find her!"

Toby is clearly excited at seeing Tammar but does as he's told and runs off to the kitchen to fetch Tammar's partner, Christine.

Tammar calls out, "Honey I'm home!"

Christine comes out from the kitchen in a pair of black Lycra tracksuit bottoms, navy blue t-shirt and yellow Marigold gloves accompanied by a trotting Toby.

"What you doing home?"

"Lovely to see you too!" He jokes.

"You know what I mean! Everything alright babes? What's in the bag?" She nods at the cigarette butts in the Ziploc bag.

"Yeah. All good. Little project I'm working on. How's the princess?" He replies.

"Yeah she's ok. She's just sleeping upstairs at the minute. You sure everything's alright?" Christine asks looking at the cigarette butts.

Tammar's thoughts are a little scattered. "Yes darling. It's all good. I need to go and see a man about a dog."

Christine is a little concerned at Tammar's surprise afternoon appearance back home when he should be working in London. Especially as she knows he enjoys working in the build up to Christmas. She asks.

"Oh yeah, who's that?"

"Alfie."

"Alfie?! You sure you know what you're doing?" She asks with a genuine note of concern in her voice. The surprise afternoon visit. Her long term fiancé looking distracted whilst holding a Ziploc bag with two cigarette butts inside and now saying he wants to go and see Alfie 'about a dog'.

Tammar still confused, replies, "Yeah, I think I do babes. I think I do. I'm going to take Toby, you never know who's watching that gaff."

"Ok my love. You sure you're ok?"

He is still very distracted in his thoughts, like he is suffering from shock. "Er, yes baby. I'm good. I'm good. I need to get going."

"Ok. Give them my best please." Christine knows he is more than capable of looking after himself but at the same time can't help but be concerned for him.

"Will do hun. I best get going before it starts getting dark. Toby Jug! Get your lead son."

Toby starts doing his excited little 'walkies' dance, spinning around and standing on his rear legs.

Tammar puts the keys to the cab, his coin dispenser and Ziploc bag with the cigarette ends down on a small table by the front door.

Christine's eye again catches the cigarette butts in the Ziploc bag.

"What you doing with them?"

"They are **very** important. **Very, very**. Whatever happens they are not to be lost, damaged, touched or in **any** way interfered with."

"Should I ask?"

"I'll explain later love I want to get going before it starts getting dark."

"Why don't you put them in the safe quickly now?"

"I don't want to disturb the princess if she's sleeping." He answers.

"You'll be fine. Do it now if they are that important."

"Ok baby. Do you have their Christmas card at hand please? It's a good prop to be seen with if anyone's watching that house."

Tammar quietly climbs the stairs and tiptoes across the landing to his and Christine's bedroom whilst looking across at a closed bedroom door with a pink 'Princess Daisy' sticker on the outside. After safely placing the Ziploc bag in the small safe in the wardrobe, he returns down to Toby who has his lead on and is holding it in his mouth and looking at the front door ready to go.

Tammar gives Christine a kiss and a quick hug. "Thank you my soul mate. See you in a couple of hours."

Tammar and Toby head off for their walk. At least that is what it is supposed to look like to anyone who might be watching Alfie's house. A neighbour innocently taking his and Alfie's dog for a walk with a chat afterwards and an exchange of Christmas cards.

Chapter 3

Abridge, Essex

Tammar and Toby walk down to the biggest house in the village. A very substantial and impressive house near to the edge of Abridge. Shielded from the view of the road by 190 feet of beautiful brick walls and iron railings behind which are thick, floral, decorative bushes and tall Leylandii conifer trees. The black entrance gates cannot be seen through and there is a sign telling of the operation of CCTV. Whoever is behind here likes their privacy and doesn't enjoy being watched.

"Crime doesn't pay but the hours are good eh Toby?!"

Tammar and Toby walk down the block paved drive and look up at a small CCTV camera on the wall and press the intercom button.

A lady's voice with an East End accent answers.

It's Alfie's wife Shirley: "Oh 'ello stranger! What can I do for you?"

Tammar leans in towards the intercom and says, "'Ello Shirl. Toby wants to know if his mate Cerberus wants to come for a walk with him?"

"Of course love. Hang on I'll buzz you in."

With that the gate remotely opens wide enough for Tammar and Toby to walk in before the gate starts to shut behind them. They walk down the block paved drive toward the modern, mock Georgian, detached house and up to the front door which opens to a smiling Shirley.

"You're looking well Tam. You never see a poor cabbie is what they say."

He smiles to himself as he glances round at their immaculate, multi million pound home that he could never afford no matter how many hours he put in as a cab driver, hands her the Christmas card and says.

"I wouldn't mind being a pound note behind you two!"

Shirley smiles. She knows exactly what he means but also knows he means nothing bad by it.

"You coming in Tam? Can I get you anything?"

"No thanks Shirl I don't want to get mud on your lovely carpets. I will need to have a chat with Alfie when I come back in half an hour if you know what I mean, if that's alright?"

"Oh it's one of those is it?"

"Yes please."

Both Shirley and Tammar know what he means by "need to have a chat". People who come to visit Alfie for "chats" have usually come to talk about criminal activity.

"Ok love. I'm sure that should be fine. I'll ask his nibs. He's doing his lengths in the pool at the moment."

She gestures with her head in the direction of their indoor swimming pool.

"He should be nearly finished. Do want to come in and wait and do it now?"

As Tammar is a close friend of the family, he is extended the offer of coming in to wait. People usually have appointments for their "chats". Some fly in from the Costa to get Alfie's advice and access to his notebook of contacts.

"After if that's alright. I've got to think a few things through but I think I've got some good news for you. How is Karen holding up?"

Shirley becomes very serious and says "Oh Tammar! My Karen! That beast! If only we could get our hands on him. She remembers very little of it. If only we could find out who it was. What we would give for that. I say to our Alf what does he want for Christmas? He's ever so quiet since it happened. He says Christmas is cancelled and he wants the head of whoever did it on a silver platter. Cerby darling!"

With that, a large menacing looking Rottweiler comes jogging out from the utility room with a large bone clamped in its jaws.

"Postman not fast enough again Cerby eh?!"
Tammar puts on a camp voice and says,
"Come on Cerby darling. Walkies! See you in half an hour babes!"
Returning to his normal voice, he says,
"Have we got a lead for Cerby? Christmas isn't cancelled Shirl. It's come early."

Chapter 4

Sub Post Offices, Balaclavas and Shotguns

For thirty minutes Tammar walks around the fields and woods with Toby and Cerberus. The two dogs make an odd couple but always seem to enjoy each other's company and get along well. They entertain each other whilst Tammar is deeply entranced in his thoughts. As he talks out loud to himself in the deserted wood to help clarify his thoughts and plans, his breath freezes under the cold winter's chill.

He mutters to himself. Sick to his stomach at what he is considering.

"It's doable. If you've got the balls to do it Tam. You've only got one life Tam. Only got one life. What about Christine and the kids? You can't leave them. Best you make sure you get it right then. Phones. Careful with phones. What doesn't speak doesn't lie."

At the end of his walk as it's time to turn back with the dogs he realises just how dark it has become. The winter's night and the absence of street lighting mean the darkness is all encompassing. Drawing a small LED torch out of his coat pocket to light the way, he realises he is left with two options. He either tells Alfie who he had in the back of his cab, the passenger's address in Chigwell and hands the matter over to Alfie who will surely kill him, or he goes with option 'B' and explains to Alfie the plan he's been mulling over these past thirty minutes.

He calls the two dogs over and squats down to put their leads on them.

"Good boys. Come here Toby. Cerberus. What would you guys do eh, if you were in my position? Do you hand it over to Alfie and say not my problem? He's *more* than capable of dealing with it. We all know that. Or do I stick my neck on the line for something which is not my fight? Poor Karen though. What a disease of a man. What are the odds of him being in my cab though? Over twenty three thousand black cabs and he gets into mine and then talks loud enough to be overheard with the intercom off.

Still undecided Tammar walks back to Alfie and Shirley's house with the two dogs, uncertain of whether to mention his big idea or just keep schtum. He thinks the plan will work. It's just a question of whether he should put his own neck on the line.

A press of the intercom on London Road, Abridge, gets the gate opening remotely once again.

Shirley stands in the doorway, "Alright Tam. Did you enjoy that Cerby darling? Come on in Tammar. Can you I get you a tea or coffee? Warm you up a bit?"

"Tea please Shirl."

Tammar takes off his muddy boots and tells Toby to be a good boy and wait in the kitchen so as not to rub his muddy belly over Alfie and Shirley's carpets.

"Don't worry Tam I'll towel off the two dogs. You go on in. His nibs is in the living room. I'll bring your tea in a minute darling."

Shirley knows from years of experience that this type of 'word' usually means business and stuff that she doesn't need, or necessarily want to know.

"Thanks Shirl."

Shirley opens the sitting room door to announce to Alfie that Tammar is here to see him. Alfie is somewhat retired these days and enjoying the easiness of country life but as Tammar believes still with connections and fingers in pies and most definitely not a man to cross.

Alfie picks up the remote control from the arm of his large, luxurious armchair and clicks off the TV.

Tammar made Alfie's acquaintance nearly 30 years ago when he used to work on the family market stall in Brick Lane in London's East End on a Sunday morning. Alfie is your archetypal, stereotypical old school East End villain. Short. Stocky. Very powerfully built and with a very thick neck. He was introduced as a man with "access to guns". A very passionate man. He was either your best friend or your worst enemy. A man who reversed the chute on a concrete mixer lorry through the window of a Rolls Royce before depositing the load of concrete into the car because the owner had upset him. But Alfie's most endearing quality back then was that he was a grandfather whose granddaughter had a very serious illness and needed expensive operations. In Alfie's own words "there isn't a sub post office around here that's safe until she has her operations" - that's a grandad. Balaclava and shotgun getting the money he needs for his sick granddaughter's operations. Unfortunately, despite many sub post offices, balaclavas and shotguns poor little Annie died. Tammar thinks that this might help with what he has in mind.

"Hello Alfie." Tammar raises his eyebrows whilst scanning around the opulent beige room and asks in a very knowing tone,

"Are we good to talk?"

"Yes son. Good to see you. What can I do for you?"

Tammar, respectfully and with sadness says,

"I heard what happened with Karen."

Pointing at the incredibly beautifully decorated Christmas tree and numerous painstakingly wrapped presents under the tree he continues,

"Shirl tells me Christmas is cancelled."

Alfie is overcome with a quiet rage. He doesn't raise his voice from his usual quiet talking volume but you know he means business.

"If I could just get my hands on that dirty jackal for what he did to my granddaughter… I don't care where he'd hide. He could hide in hell and I'd walk straight in with a meat cleaver, shit them *all* up. I would introduce him to pain that was unthought of in all the nine circles of hell. You understand what I'm saying son?"

Tammar nods his silent understanding of the type of retribution that awaits her attacker. Hell would be scared if Alfie came in with a temper.

Tammar removes a couple of oversized cushions from the armchair opposite Alfie, places them on the sofa and takes a seat.

"Her and her bloody cushions! What is it with that woman! You can't sit down for bloody cushions!" says Alfie. He can say it but no one else dare criticise his adored wife who he puts on a pedestal.

Tammar starts to talk. "You'll never guess who I had in the back of my cab today, gassing away about what he's done?"

Alfie just gestures with his hand not quite sure if Tammar is still on the same subject as the attack on Karen.

"You know how they talk and forget about the guy in the front of the cab."

Alfie quickly becomes a little annoyed and impatient at Tammar's apparent insensitivity. "Yeah, what you saying Son?"

"I had the guy who hurt your Karen."

Alfie's eyes lit up. "Good boy. Certain?"

"Oh yeah, he was on his mobile talking about what he did and how he did it and it **had** to be your Karen. Said it had made the BBC news website?"

Alfie sat up in his seat. "Did you get where he worked? Take him home? What do you have for me? I'll send some nutters from Parkhurst, go round and collect him!"

"I took him to his home. Multi million pound mansion of a gaff, bigger than this. Brand new Maserati and an Audi TT parked up outside. He's minted! I picked him up from his jewellers shop in Knightsbridge by the Park Tower hotel at the Seville Street rank. His wife answered the door although she looks sick of the sight of him. He comes across as a despicable example of an animal. It sounds like he is a multiple serial rapist with possibly a hundred victims."

Alfie's eyes opened wide as if to say, "Really?!"

Tammar continued. "I've got the registration plates of the two motors parked on the drive. I'm sure with your contacts we could get his name etc."

"You give me that address Tam, he's a dead man walking." Seething anger became etched in the deep, passionate wrinkles on Alfie's brow and whilst still talking quietly, just the tone in his voice and the fixed look of certainty in his eyes scared Tammar. Even Shirley, Cerberus and Toby outside of the room started to be a bit concerned. Shirley stopped in her tracks with the tray of teas and a plate of biscuits outside the sitting room door and didn't dare bring it in to disturb them.

"Oooh! Serious one." she whispered to herself and the dogs as they looked quizzically up at her.

Tammar reached into his pocket and produced the taxi receipt with the registration numbers of the two cars on it.

"I overheard him say that in Africa they call him Mzungu. Turns out he's a neighbour."

Alfie's anger and volume suddenly shot up. "**What! Dirty Marcus?!**"

"No, no. I mean Chigwell. Just down the road. How about you don't send the nutters? We leave him."

Alfie, almost incredulous at what he was hearing angrily spat out.

"**Come again?!**"

"Hear me out. I've got something I think you'll like more."

If Tammar didn't know Alfie very well he wouldn't dare push him beyond this point.

"Go on but this **best** be good." Alfie's patience was starting to wear thin.

"I'd like your blessing and a little bit of help with your Hatton Garden connection but instead of just killing him now how about this…" Tammar goes on to explain what he's planning.

After about an hour the two of them rise from their armchairs and Alfie smiles and motions with open arms for Tammar to give him a hug.

"You're a good boy Tam, from good stock. You're sure you can do all this and you don't need me to put together a team for you?"

"No thanks Alfie. I mean I've yet to approach them but as I say each one should be sympathetic to our cause for one reason or another. If any of them blows out I'll need to come back to you and your Yellow Pages contacts but if they all say yes then this way none of them know each other. I'm the only link holding them all together and they are all straight men, without records. We should be good. I will need your help with that burglar though.

"No problem. I know an old cat burglar used to work the jewellers of Bond Street through the roofs. Your job should be like delivering Milk Tray chocolates to him. He owes me a favour. Do you think you've got enough time for your little one though, that little Twinkle/Treacle, my little princess?"

Tammar takes a sharp breath in. "That I don't know. Maybe a prayer to the man upstairs on that one."

By now Alfie's temper had long calmed down and he spoke more as a concerned friend and father-like figure. "Six months could be cutting it a bit fine and then with travelling… You can make big plans but if they take a turn for the worse then it all goes down the pan at the last minute. I know, I've been there."

"Six months, fingers crossed. I've got to research some stuff and pull it all together but I'm thinking six months," said Tammar.

"Well son, you have my blessing. I'll fill Tizer in closer to the time when all is set. Sounds like a good plan. You're wasted being a cabbie, wasted you are!"

"Thanks Alfie, your blessing and help means the world to me and you're sure you're ok with the prize?"

Alfie nods. "Take your time. Double check everything. Don't tell no-one anything they don't need to know. See it through like you've described to me and with a bit of luck it comes off. Have your escape route planned in case it all goes tits up."

"Thank you."

Alfie becomes serious once again. "Remember loose lips sink ships"

"Ok. Mum's the word."

Tammar walks to and opens the sitting room door to find Shirley in the hall with the two dogs.

"Thanks for that tea Shirl!" he says in a joking sarcastic tone.

As he goes to leave the room, Alfie's strong grip grasps Tammar by the upper arm and stops him dead in his tracks. He thinks he's about to be given a stern warning by this old school villain of the East End or hear him talk about the old East End wall of silence of years ago.

Tammar looks worriedly at Shirley as if to say, 'what have I done wrong?!'

"You didn't say what you thought of Shirley's Christmas tree?!"

Tammar breathes a sigh of relief and lets out a little nervous laugh.

"Oh it's gorgeous Shirl. Every year you out do yourself. I thought you said Christmas was cancelled Alfie?!"

"Shirl! Thanks to this boy Christmas is back on!"

Keen to now get out of the house Tammar says, "Come on Toby get your lead son!"

Alfie now smiling for the first time since the attack on Karen, looks at Shirley and says, "Love that boy!"

Tammar leaves with Toby the dog so Alfie can explain to Shirley that they have found the man who attacked their granddaughter Karen.

As Tammar and Toby approach the black gate, they can hear Shirley shouting,

"What?!"

With that the front door bursts open and Shirley comes running out in her carpet slippers towards Tammar, throws her arms around him and gives him a kiss on the cheek and a big hug.

"God bless you Tammar! God bless you! Alfie's just told me."

"What?! All of it?"

"No, he just said you found him and you're going to get him back and that you had a good plan."

"Yeah, I think we might have something."

In a rare show, Shirley's exterior façade slips just momentarily and you can see that like attracts like and she is a perfect wife for Alfie.

"You get him for me Tam. You understand me? You get him for me!"

"He's gonna pay Shirl. He's gonna pay. One way or another, he's gonna pay."

She clasps his hands in hers and looks him deep in the eyes with gratitude and kisses him once again on the cheek.

"Thank you! You're a very good boy Tam! Father Christmas will have something for you!" She says wagging a knowing finger up in the air to the side of her head.

"Go on! Get back in before you catch a cold!"

His 'auntie' turns and runs back to Alfie who is watching from the doorway. The two of them hug and wave to Tammar and Toby as the gates open to let them out. Tammar waves goodbye. It's good news all round.

Now he's got to walk back to his house and explain to his Christine why he's not currently at work driving the cab. This one might take a bit more selling…

Chapter 5

Pensioner Mick, Terry, Roger, Tizer and the Milk Tray Man

Once again, Tammar speaks to us the reader:

"Now as I've said, in my time I've worked at many different jobs, heard many different and interesting life stories and anecdotes and half learnt some very interesting things. I can't remember a conversation with my missus from ten days ago but some little nugget of information from twenty or thirty years ago - no problem."

Take our first geezer Mick. Mick is seventy-eight years old, five foot eight, quite solidly built and as game as they come. I worked with him in the Home Office about twenty-two years ago. He is real old London. Comes from the East Street area just off the Walworth Road in South London. Worked in the Navy as a lad. Boxed at amateur level. He developed tinnitus when I knew him. Had a constant ringing in his ears from the boxing and had to start wearing hearing aids which he wasn't keen on because they used to whistle. He used to turn them off, couldn't always hear the conversation around him, then he would turn them back on and you would have to repeat whatever you said for him a second time.

He was looking to get pensioned off from the Home Office when one day an opportunity presented itself. There were some builders in doing odd jobs in the office block we worked in. He noticed that they had left a length of two-by-four wood across the entrance to the gents' toilet. He went in and as he came out he somersaulted over the wood as if he had tripped, and landed flat on his back. "I can't move! I can't move!" He never worked another day in his life and good luck to him. He got paid out and pensioned off.

He's married to his childhood sweetheart, Jean, who he adores. They met in their early twenties. She means the world to him and him to her. Theirs is an eternal love that makes you believe in marriage.

Now, before Mick joined the Home Office he had a career working down the sewers. Dirty work but the money and hours were good apparently. I think it became a bit too much like hard work as he got older. When I joined the Home Office, despite the age gap between the two of us, we were very good friends. I had a lot of time and respect for Mick.

He trusted me and I, him. He told me one time about this plan he had but never pulled off, of robbing Johnson Matthey the gold bullion dealers. Apparently they had been inside the building doing work when the idea came to him. Because of his knowledge of the sewer system running under Johnson Matthey he wanted to go back into the building, get a tennis ball on a chain with a screw and a hook on the other end. Screw the hook into a gold bar as they are soft. Drop it into the sewer where he had already worked out how he could go and collect it as the tennis ball would float showing him where the gold bar was hidden.

As I say, he never carried it out and he lives on his old age pension now. I never could quite work out how much the missed opportunity bothered him; maybe a little, maybe a lot. I don't know but I think he will be receptive to my approach for a number of reasons and his area of expertise will prove invaluable.

Our next geezer is Terry. Now Terry is my brother in law, lives down in Surrey. Forty years old and naturally a very big, strong man. Like most of nature's giants, he's as quiet and gentle and laid back as they come. Don't you find that though? The big guys know they can. They've got nothing to prove to themselves. There is an inner calm and peace. It's always the little guys with the big yap. Out to prove something to themselves. Little man syndrome. They are the little yappy Jack Russell's of life. The huge, big dog - one bark a week. Woof! That's it! The little dog, yap, yap, yap all day long. And so it is with Tel. Laid back to the point of being horizontal. Bit of a worrier at times though. That could be a problem.

He's currently in the building game. I say currently as he used to work at a fireworks company along with his dad. Not their company but they worked together. The company folded and now he's labouring.

One time he was talking about his work at the fireworks company and he said how the boss of the company was driving round with a piece of C4 explosive in the door well of his van and that it was safe until you put a detonator in it.

He went on to say how, you know like when you're at work sometimes and you get a little bored, you play around with stuff a bit? Well apparently it's the same thing even if you work with fireworks. So, what do you do? Well, turns out you start messing around with explosives. Packing them into containers for a bigger bang. He said they blew up a caravan with a 50p coin sized piece of C4. Imagine that! That big! Apparently the key is to pack your explosives into a container and then suspend it in the air. I've heard that said by a couple of old ex bomb disposal guys I knew too.

When I give him the back story and tell him what I'm planning I think he will be receptive to my approach and his specialist knowledge will prove invaluable too.

The third guy I want is Roger. Roger is about 5 foot 6 inches tall and about the same in circumference around the waist.

Roger I used to know when I worked under the railway arches down Jarrow Road in Bermondsey years ago.

Before I met him he used to work for Westminster Council driving skip lorries. I think he got laid off and got a bit of redundancy money. He went on to pursue his dream of racing offshore powerboats. I remember the sponsorship deals always seemed a problem for him. That and his weight. Being a professional offshore powerboat racer and a fat fucker at the same time was a bit of a problem.

He used to have an industrial plastic wheelie bin to act as a water tank. He would strip the engines of the powerboats down and rebuild them. He said to properly test the engines he wanted the propellers in water hence the industrial plastic wheelie bin filled with water. We'd be working in our arch down the far end of Jarrow Road and then above all the other noise would be this absolute beast of an engine noise being tested. Excellent! But to take the

urther he said that he really wanted to have the whole boat in
ɔr that he used to take these proper offshore powerboats on the
Th̲e̲ ar in as Tower Bridge. I asked him once about the river police and
he said, "That's alright. There's no fucker on the river who can catch me." Fair
point methinks.

Our paths went in different directions and I haven't seen Roger in many,
many years but I imagine he's still a fat fucker with a fast as fuck offshore powerboat tucked away somewhere. Knowing a little about his and his wife's story
I'm going to guess that he will be up for it too.

The next guy would be Tizer. He won't know what he's doing or why but
he'll do it and he'll never speak of it to anyone. He's got that old East End 'wall
of silence' attitude to him despite only being twenty five years old.

Also crucial to our whole plan is Alfie's Milk Tray Man.

And I learnt the other day that Alfie has got the name of our guy from
his contacts who were able to do a Police National Computer search with the
registration numbers from the cars in Chigwell.

Turns out our Rohypnol dropping, serial rapist, diamond smuggler is
called Simon Rosenstein and is married to Louise.

Chapter 6

A Meeting at The Dell

Monday the 10th June, 2013. 7.15am. Tammar and Terry have agreed to meet Mick at The Dell, at the end of the Serpentine Lake in Hyde Park at 7.15am with strict instructions for no-one to be late. As they get closer they can see Mick standing out in his white Microgard coveralls and black Century 4000 Super Safety thigh waders. He has on a white hard hat with an LED head torch. Underneath the hard hat he is wearing an extra close mesh blue Lion brand hairnet keeping his fine grey hair concealed. On his back he has a small black Adidas backpack over his body harness. He is wearing thick red rubber gloves and over his shoulder is a strap for his large fifteen million candlepower torch which rests on his hip. He stands there looking very happy with himself, holding a 5 foot tall by 1.5 inch diameter prise bar in his left hand.

Tammar and Terry are dressed in the same white Microgard coveralls and black Century 4000 Super Safety thigh waders, white hard hats, thick red rubber gloves and body harnesses. They don't have a prise bar or torch but they have on their backs larger rucksacks, which you can tell are full of kit.

As they get closer Terry says, "You know when you said he was old and a pensioner?"

"Yeah?"

"Oh good Lord Tam! How old is he?!" Terry starts off loud and excited but finishes the sentence in more hushed tones as they continue to get closer to a smiling Mick.

Whispering under his breath Terry says to Tammar,

"He's bloody ancient Tam! He looks like fucking Gandalf standing there with that prise bar!"

"Shhh! He'll hear you if his hearing aids are switched on."

"Hearing aids! Are you 'aving a laugh?!"

As they get closer pensioner Mick turns and smiles from ear to ear, eager to start his adventure. He can't quite focus on their faces yet even with his glasses but two people dressed identically to him walking through Hyde Park - this has to be them.

As Tam and Terry's faces gradually come into focus Mick just raises his right palm and nods his head. Tam and Terry return the gesture.

He says, "Grey and overcast but forecast to be dry at least. It's supposed to warm up a bit later. Shall we begin gentlemen?"

A little hesitantly, Terry grips Tammar by the upper arm from behind and says.

"One moment please. Can I just have a quick word Tam, over here?"

After a short walk and turning their backs to to Mick, Tammar asks,

"What's up?"

"Seriously?! This guy?! Tam…"

Tammar quickly interrupts him. "No names remember!"

"Sorry. Son! But seriously he's about 90 surely!?"

"78"

"78! He should be at home eating Werther's Originals not playing young men's games! What if something happens to him today? I swear the Grim Reaper should be standing next to him holding a scythe and looking at his watch 'Not much longer for you old man.' "

"He's already agreed we leave him behind if the worst should come to the worst. He doesn't link back to me through phone records or anything like that and he's real old school. They would never get a peep out of him. He reckons prison would be better than being on a pension at his age anyway. He's essential to today Big Man, just as much as me or you. Today needs many parts to make it happen and everyone is here for a reason. Him included. Trust me on this one."

Terry looks back at this pensioner in his thick rimmed, old glasses and doubts his capabilities for such an adventure but trusts his brother-in-law's judgement.

"Ok. Ok. But if today goes wrong because of him I'm holding you personally responsible 'Son'".

"Trust me he's golden. I'm shitting myself about today just as I imagine you are. I can't wait to get down and get the manhole cover closed behind us and we're out of sight. If truth be told I've had countless bad dreams about it in the build up to today. The closer we've got the more frequent the bad dreams have become. I don't want to go to prison. I bet out of the three of us he's the coolest of the lot. Look at him!"

Tammar and Terry glance over at pensioner Mick who is casually looking around at the different plants, trees, flowers and passers-by in the park. He even gives a little smile, a nod and a wink to two twenty something Spanish girls that walk past.

"Hola!"

They giggle and smile back.

"See? Come on!" Tammar says in a reassuring voice, "It'll be fine."

With a reluctant shrug of his shoulders the big man nods his agreement and the two of them walk the few steps back to Mick.

"Alright Champ?"

"Yes Son! I've been looking forward to today."

"*He's* not been losing sleep." Terry says dryly.

The three of them are beside a little gate in Hyde Park, at a small fenced off wooded area at the bottom of the Dell at the end of the Serpentine Lake next to Rotten Row. The little gate has a 'FB' (fire brigade) padlock and chain securing it.

"You want to do the honours Champ?" Tammar asks Mick.

They have agreed in the planning of this to not use their real names but nicknames instead in case they are overheard. Mick is 'Champ' from his boxing days. Terry is 'Big Man' for obvious reasons and Tammar is 'Son' after Mick's natural father-like affection for him.

Mick pulls out a bunch of six fire brigade keys and selects the small FB1 padlock key. He unlocks the gate and the three of them enter.

Fire brigade locks are used where quick access is required by the fire brigade and other emergency services. They are standard locks with only a few different key variations and so Mick's bunch of six keys will see them through the day.

In the corner of the Dell is a large, raised manhole cover discretely hidden amongst the trees.

Tammar turns and addresses Mick and Terry, "Are you both sure you want to go through with this? It's ok if you want to back out. No-one's forcing anyone. We've done nothing criminal yet."

Mick is the first to speak up.

"Son, I've the least to lose. I've got my Jean but probably not many years left. Old Father Time favours no man. I think today is sure going to beat shopping at the supermarket or going to the bookies. I'm in!"

"Tel?"

"I'm in Tam. Let's get going. We're on the clock here. Let's go before the groundskeepers come back or the parks police come along, or the tide comes back in, or the weather forecast is wrong and it starts bucketing down with rain while we're in the tunnels and we drown. I don't like the look of those clouds."

Tammar curls the corner of his lip in a sarcastic manner and whilst looking at Mick nods at Terry and says, "Always the 'appy camper isn't he!"

Mick agrees with Terry. "Yeah, let's not hang about. Let's get going. Once inside be very careful at all times. The flow will change from light to strong. The depth will change from shallow to deep. Whilst you should be able to see through the water only walk in the water. The sides will be slippery. There will be silt build up. One time it will take your weight, the next it will gently give out underneath you."

Tammar takes off his large rucksack and places it on the ground for Terry to pull out a pair of bolt croppers.

Terry lines up the short blades of the bolt croppers with the shackle of the padlock to the manhole cover and with an effortless press of the long handles, the croppers snip through the padlock.

Mick has a cheeky grin on his face at Terry's obvious display of strength by cutting through the padlock so effortlessly.

"Someone's had their Weetabix this morning. He's a big un' alright Tam!"

Terry places the remains of the padlock into a Ziploc bag and returns it and the bolt croppers to Tammar's large rucksack.

While this was going on Tammar has pulled out a large, sealed, clear 'evidence' bag with a Dubarry Wexford, walnut coloured, leather Wellington boot inside.

"Here you are Champ. £350 quids worth of welly! What do you reckon then?"

Mick can't believe what he's hearing. He splutters out,

"£350?! For a welly?! It is nice - I'll give him that!"

Tammar nods to Terry who opens the manhole cover. Tammar takes off his large thick red rubber gloves to reveal he is wearing a pair of latex gloves underneath. Using a pair of scissors he cuts open the sealed evidence bag and pulls out the boot. The sole and heel are covered in dried mud and soil. He takes the boot and puts his hand and arm inside.

"You two go first. We don't want to disturb this."

They all switch on their LED head torches.

Mick says, "I'll go down first. You wait until the guy in front of you is clear of the ladder then he calls up. That way no one falls and lands on the guy in front."

Mick goes down the hole first. Once clear of the initial ladder he calls up to Terry.

"Okay Big Man!"

With Mick and Terry safely down and getting the call to come down himself, Tammar wipes the dry mud off the sole of the Dubarry boot onto the rim of the manhole. He returns it to the evidence bag and puts it back in the rucksack which he drops down for Terry to catch.

A quick check of his wristwatch reveals it's 7.20am and down he goes closing the heavy, dirty, rusty manhole cover behind him. Pieces of crud fall down the back of the neck of his coveralls.

Instead of one ladder going straight down as you might expect, there is a flight of brick stairs covered in thick congealed fat which leads sideways onto the river underneath them.

Once Tammar has carefully descended these rarely used steps into a hidden subterranean realm of London, Mick passes him the fifteen million candlepower torch.

There is a loud banging noise from the distant blackness ringing through the tunnel. Tammar and Terry exchange concerned glances.

Tammar switches on the fifteen million candlepower torch which lights up far down the tunnel. The banging noise happens again. They now realise it must be traffic going over a manhole cover further down towards The Egg underneath the Knightsbridge road.

They convene at the bottom of the stairs before stepping into the water. Mick is in charge at this stage. He holds out Tammar's rucksack in exchange for the fifteen million candlepower torch. He speaks first.

"Ok. Have we all got our eyes used to the darkness down here? I'm going to switch this torch off and we're going to have to rely on our head torches. As good as this big boy is it's only good for 20 minutes and then the battery will be flat plus it gets as hot as the sun if you leave it switched on. So from now on head torches only unless we really need the big one. Ok?"

"Ok Mick. Shit! Sorry Champ! Champ! Sorry I meant Champ!"

"That's ok Son but just all of us remember it's nicknames only. We should be alone down here but we don't need to be overheard giving our names away."

Mick familiarises Tammar and Terry as they are probably all turned around and more than likely have lost their bearings in the darkness of the tunnel. Pointing upstream first he says.

"Ok. The Serpentine is that way and this is the flow from the end of The Dell water feature. We are now standing in the river Westbourne. We're about 310 metres in the opposite direction downstream to The Egg where we will meet the Storm Relief. We will be in the Westbourne at this level and the Storm Relief will be running underneath us from left to right. We will pass straight over it like we are crossing the road. The Storm Relief will continue along underneath the A4 Knightsbridge road and do a left at Harvey Nicks then go down Sloane Street. When we get to The Egg you will be able to look down and see the Storm Relief flowing underneath us. When we walk above it just be very careful. The Westbourne comes down to a pinch point and becomes very fast flowing. If you get knocked off your feet you could go arse over tit and fall into the Storm Relief below and it's broken back time and would ruin today and all the planning. It will be noisy and dangerous. Walk where I walk. Take it easy and look after each other. Walk two metres apart to stop from splashing the guy in front. Once safely past The Egg, matey's shop will be just the other side. I will need to pace out a further 15 paces to line up with the alcoves in the basement of Cloacina jewellers."

Terry raises his hand to ask a question…

"Why is it called The Egg where the river and the Storm Relief pass over each other?"

"You'll see in a minute; it's shaped like an egg. We are up here like on a flyover and the Storm Relief will pass underneath. The brick work around the two is shaped like an egg."

Terry raises his hand a second time:

"What's the score with rats down here?"

Mick chuckles at the big man raising his hand like a child.

"The first guy will more than likely scare them away and they'll disappear into some crack in the wall. You should be ok. Don't worry."

They offer each other a helping hand as they take their first steps into the river and feel the water pushing against their Wellington boots around their ankles. Tammar gazes at the tiny water molecules suspended in the moist air slowly floating towards him. They create a mesmerising effect as they move towards him. He can't tell how close they are as they continue to get closer and closer.

"Son!" Mick calls out.

"Huh? Oh! Right! With you!" Tammar snaps out of it and comes back to reality.

They start to walk, keeping Mick's suggested two metres apart. Mick takes the lead and the three start to walk underneath Rotten Row, South Carriage Drive and exit Hyde Park under Albert Gate in-between the French and Kuwait embassies.

As they get closer they can hear the roar of the Storm Relief passing in front of them as it flows underneath the A4 Knightsbridge road and the occasional banging of the manhole cover as vehicles drive overhead.

Tammar pulls out a smartphone and points at a map on the screen.

"We're here Champ. A4 Knightsbridge. Kuwait embassy. French embassy. Albert Gate."

Mick points at the sign on the wall behind him, "I know Son."

The Egg. River Westbourne flowing over the Storm Relief.

Mick points down at the Storm Relief flowing underneath them and has to raise his voice a little to be heard.

"That's the Storm Relief, running underneath us now. The A4 Knightsbridge road is above us. It flows down to Harvey Nicks on the corner and does a left down Sloane Street. I just need to pace out from here to line up with the alcoves in the basement of the shop."

Terry puts his forearm up to his nose;

"Bloody hell! It doesn't half pen and ink!"

Mick ignores Terry's protests of the smell and silently looks around to get his bearings; once he feels happy that he understands where he is corresponding to street level he carefully counts fifteen paces and touches the wall with his left palm.

"Here. Here will be the third alcove. William Street above us. Alcove 3 here."

"You sure?" asks Tammar.

Mick points up. "Tree roots. He's got an Alder tree outside his shop by the clock. In 2010 it was subject to a planning enquiry when it was proposed to remove it as it had outgrown its current location, and replace it with a silver birch. Don't worry I've had a good snoop around at street level quite a few times Son."

"You're the boss Champ. Let's see what this bad boy can do."

Terry turns his back to Tammar so that from out of his rucksack he can pull Terry's homemade shape charge explosive ring and hand it to him.

Tammar says to Mick, "Ok Champ, time for your dream to become a reality."

With an excited glint in his eye Mick says, "Let's do it Son!"

Terry attaches the shape charge to the tunnel wall.

"I hope you two appreciate this is Special Forces level of expertise here?"

Tammar and Mick roll their eyes at each other in an OTT manner. Both realise the skill involved in what Terry is about to do but neither can pass up the possibility of teasing him about it.

Mick says, "You want to see Special Forces level of expertise then pull my finger! No?" With that Mick lets out a loud fart that echoes around the tunnel.

"Ah jeez!"

"Good God man! Did you follow through?"

The old pensioner slips his false teeth half out and gurns back at them.

If Mick's calculations are correct the third alcove in the basement of the shop will be on the other side of this wall.

"Ok. Take cover Champ. Son, get behind me."

The three men move into position either side of the explosive ring. Terry reckons front or back is taking the hit - standing to either side is going to be safe.

View of the alcove from inside Simon Rosenstein's Cloacina
jewellers extending under the pavement.

Terry glances at both Mick and Tammar and back to Mick again.

"Ready?"

Mick gives a knowing quick nod, switches off his two hearing aids, gives a silent double thumbs up and puts his hands over his ears.

Tammar checks his wristwatch once more - 7.33am, and turns his back to the explosives, covers both ears as Terry standing next to him presses the detonator button with his right thumb.

Boom!

Bricks and rubble go flying into the water. Smoke fills the tunnel for a while. Tammar and Terry choke on the thick dust and start coughing but nothing can be heard from Mick. Neither Terry nor Tammar can see Mick just a few feet away on the other side.

Tammar is the first to speak.

"Christ! You weren't mucking about was you?! Champ you still there?"

A silence lingers in the tunnel. No answer comes back from inside the smoke filled tunnel. Tammar starts to wonder what on earth he's going to tell Mick's wife Jean…

The smoke starts to clear and Mick's white coverall once again starts to become visible.

Tammar asks: "You ok?"

Mick gestures with one finger meaning one moment. He turns both his hearing aids back on.

"About half past four" he jokes. "I'm good Son but I think someone might have knocked at the front door" as he gestures to the hole in the wall they have just made.

The smoke clears some more and you can see straight into the basement of Cloacina jewellers.

The three of them wait patiently in the running water listening for the sound of any alarms going off. There doesn't appear to be any. Just the sound of the water and the occasional vehicle hitting the manhole cover above. They smile very proud, broad smiles. Mick hands Tammar a three hole balaclava from out of his backpack which he pulls over his head. He is consumed by both fear and excitement although he doesn't want Mick or Terry to spot his fear. He swallows nervously and takes a few precarious steps over the pile of bricks through the alcove shaped hole they have just created in the tunnel wall and steps into the basement of the shop whilst Mick and Terry continue to wait outside.

His head torch picks out a cloudy haze of dust hanging in the air. A few more steps and he exits the alcove and looks up at the ceiling.

The glass tiles in the pavement on William Street can be seen overhead. He looks into the second and first alcoves; no sign of any safes.

He enters the first 'room' of the basement and there in the far left corner are the two safes. He quickly tiptoes into the second room and checks the stairs up to the main shop. No sign of any life or movement up there. He checks his wristwatch once more: 7.36am, and thinks they still have two hours before the first of the staff arrive. The alarms of the shop are not going off either. All is good. The light from his head torch catches a glimpse of a bank of light switches. He carefully reads the labels above each individual switch and turns on the three switches for the basement lighting, being careful to not touch the ones marked 'shop'. He quickly jogs on his tiptoes back to the hole in the wall at the end of alcove three where a figure wearing a 3 hole balaclava, white hard hat and head torch is looking in.

The voice from the balaclava is pensioner Mick.

"Why you tiptoeing round like a fairy? If they didn't hear that boom they're not going to hear you walking around down here are they? How've we done Son?"

Returning to flat feet Tammar says.

"Absolutely spot on! Perfect Champ. Well done! It was just as you said it would be. We're in but you're never going to believe it."

The old man practically gasps with excitement.

"What? What is it?!"

Tammar gestures with his hand…

"Come and see for yourself."

He extends out a helping hand to steady Mick as he climbs over the pile of bricks and rubble into the basement.

The basement is now fully lit as all the fluorescent tubes are now illuminated. The two of them walk into room one.

Mick's mouth drops open.

"No wonder he got robbed! Look! Can you believe it?! What a prat!"

There in the corner of the room are the two safes - neither door closed or locked. Sparkling like the contents of Aladdin's cave, trays of loose diamonds. Some polished and plenty more rough cut. Still others in brick shaped packages unopened. Plus the jewellery trays from the window displays.

Mick can't believe his eyes.

"He's done our work for us."

Tammar replies, "I never wanted to go upstairs anyway and then it dawned on me. What do they do when they remove the window displays - put them in the safes."

It almost looked as if there might be a slight tear of pride and joy in the corner of Mick's eye behind his balaclava as his dreams of robbing Johnson Matthey the bullion dealers, the phone calls to Thames Water, the Environment Agency and Westminster Council's planning departments plus his years of working down the sewers had all been worthwhile.

Tammar is still concerned about the noise the explosion made.

"Are you sure we're ok? I mean we've just set off a bomb in Knightsbridge between the French and Kuwait embassies. We're not going to start a war or get people running to investigate are we?"

With a knowing look and the air of quiet confidence of someone who definitely knows what they are talking about Mick replies,

"What do you do when you hear a loud bang?"

There is a pause as Tammar can't think of an answer.

Stumped by his question Mick provides the answer.

"I'll tell you. You wait for the second one. You say "what was that?" and you wait for the second one to do something about it. If there is no second one you just leave it."

With that, a very bright torch shines straight into their eyes and dazzles them. A loud, authoritative voice says, **"Gotcha! What's going on here then?!"**

The beam of light from the torch goes out of their eyes to reveal it is Terry wearing his balaclava and playing silly games with Mick's fifteen million candle power torch.

Tammar is scared and relieved in an instant.

"Argh! Good God man don't do that!"

With that, 78 year old Mick grabs at his heart with his face contorted in absolute agony, lets out a gasp of air and goes down on both knees with his chin dropping to his chest.

Tammar and Terry flash terrified glances at each other!

Tammar quickly kneels down at Mick's side grabbing the top of his arm, "Champ?!"

Mick's head slowly lifts and his hand unclamps from around his heart,

"Only joking! Two can play at that game!"

Terry's relief alone is worth the practical joke, "Oh good grief!"

Tammar rises back to his feet.

"You coffin dodging old…"

The three laugh.

Tammar extends out a helping hand which Mick pulls heavily on to get back to his feet.

"Come on! Get up! There's work to be done.

Tammar nods at Mick and says to Terry, "The old boy was absolutely spot on and your rig worked perfect! It was as easy as you said it would be. 'Your wish is my command' - Aladdin's cave."

Now it's Terry's turn to gasp open mouthed at the fortune in the two safes…

"You couldn't make it up. Two safes, neither one locked over the weekend and they're filled with diamonds. What a mug! How did you know it would be this easy to blow our way into his basement Mick - sorry, I mean Champ?"

Mick replies, "Back in the day it was common to have basement access to the sewers where you could sling your human waste in. You would have carried your slop bucket to the basement and thrown it into the river here. When Bazelgette unified the system in the Victorian era this would have been sealed off, if it hadn't been already at that stage. It would have just been bricked up. All we've done is help them open it up again."

Tammar had to admit to himself the simple genius of Mick's solution to his original problem.

"I must admit, to start off with I started researching thermic lances, thinking we would have to burn our way in. But they would have required oxygen tanks and it was just a no go. You really could not have asked for this to have been designed better for us could you? So, Big Man, does this answer your question "Why aren't we just walking in through the front door with balaclavas and shotguns and robbing the strunt?" Because he'd do all our work for us. Yeah, there's far more wealth down here than there is left in the showcases in the shop upstairs I bet. I guess he thought the security is all at the front of the shop with the double security doors, doorman, alarms and CCTV and that's why we're not going upstairs or using real names here. Nicknames only remember. Champ can you give us the little backpack please?"

With that Mick takes off his small, black Adidas backpack and passes it to Tammar who pours the trays of loose polished diamonds into a clear evidence bag and seals it up. He then puts all of the uncut diamonds and brick shaped packages into another evidence bag and seals that up. The jewellery is sealed into a third evidence bag. All three bags are put into the backpack, which is then passed back to Mick for him to put on.

"All good. Let's scarper."

Tel goes first followed by Mick; they now wait in the running water of the Westbourne for Tammar to appear which he does eight seconds later. Terry and Mick go to take off their balaclavas.

Tammar exclaims, "Wait!"

He squats down on the pile of bricks just inside the shop, slips his rucksack off and pulls out the two evidence bags, each containing a Dubarry Wexford Wellington boot. As he is not wearing his thick rubber gloves at this stage and only wearing latex gloves he puts a hand and arm in either boot, walks into the Westbourne and crouches down enough to put both boots in the flow of water making sure that the waterproof leather has the water flow all around it. Then he takes the wet boots back into the basement of the shop and deliberately makes some footprints in the right hand corner of the room.

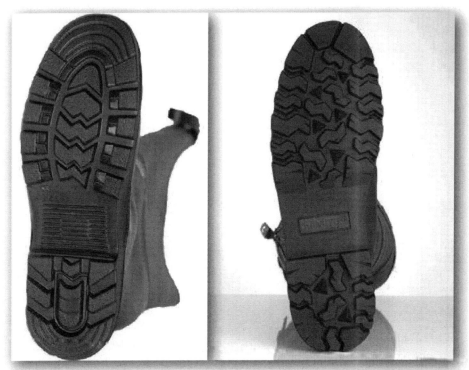

Century 4000 thigh wader sole on left/Dubarry Wexford on right.

He comes back out into the Westbourne once more and squelches the soles of the boots in tunnel mud and muck before carefully returning the boots to two new individual, large evidence bags. Seals them up and places them upright in his rucksack and puts it on his back. He exits over the pile of bricks back into the Westbourne and once clear from the hole pulls off his hard hat and balaclava and says,

"God! That was easier than we dared thought wasn't it? Didn't even lock his bloody safes over the weekend. Surely that must invalidate his insurance? Ok. Let's get the hell out of here. Same as before. Me, Champ close to me and Big Man close behind Champ. Slowest is quickest. No one slips over. Nothing gets lost."

"How we doing for time Son?"

"Let's see. It's now 7.45 which makes us ten minutes ahead of schedule! Bonus!"

Mick and Terry remove their balaclavas and the three men start off on their downstream walk through the tunnel toward the Thames. Water flow in the tunnel is fairly constant throughout. They've waited many months for low summer water in the river and the tides of the Thames. By using charts of tide times from the Port of London authority, they were able to best predict a day and time for doing this.

Tammar, feeling the need to make conversation after a few minutes of silence says,

"This walking in water is harder than you'd think. I'm breaking a sweat here."

Eventually they make it to the pipe above Sloane Square station but before they can access it they are confronted by a closed, heavy steel flap which has just a small 'cat flap' at the bottom to allow the water to flow through.

Tammar turns and asks Mick: "How do we get past that?"

"It's ok. They are designed to flow one way, downstream to the Thames. This is why we started at Knightsbridge and worked our way down instead of starting at the Thames and trying to work our way up. If we were trying to open it from the other side we'd have a right job on our hands."

Terry hands over the 5 foot prise bar he's been carrying all morning to Mick who sticks the end in the corner of the flap and gestures to Terry to put his weight on the heavy steel flap.

"Come on then big'un!"

The two of them work on the heavy steel flap but it won't budge. They try and try again but it won't move. There is a very uncomfortable silence in the tunnel as the three men stop and exchange looks at each other.

Tammar tries to conceal his fear and being the leader is the first to break the silence.

"What's happening Champ?"

Mick replies, "She's stuck fast. There was always a possibility of this happening."

Terry starts to lose it, "Trapped?! No! No! No! No! **No!**"

Chapter 7
Trapped Like Rats

T ammar feigns composure and tries to keep everyone calm.

"Alright. Cool like the Fonz. What's the solution Champ? We can't go back. Staff could have come in early and be discovering the raid as we speak. We run the risk that our one explosion *was* investigated by the Diplomatic Protection Police and they're always tooled up with shooters under the back-seats of their red cars. The park could be swarming with Old Bill and we can't pop up from the sewer like we've seen nothing with millions of pounds of diamonds on us. We *must* go forward. We're trapped like rats unless we can go forward."

Terry scared and a little angry, chips in at what he sees as the pensioner's fault.

"Didn't you check our exit before we committed to today?!"

Mick very calmly and matter-of-factly considering the gravity of the situation, replies:

"Everything was checked but I didn't dare come down here on my own beforehand. It's too dangerous to go draining on your own. It's probably sat shut since the day it was installed. It could just be silt and fat build up."

Mick very calmly starts to jab away at the silt and fat build up at the bottom of the flap and then drags the heavy prise bar along the bottom where the flap and the tunnel meet.

The big man is starting to panic.

"Come on! We've got an escape planned. It will all be ruined if we can't get this thing moving. You especially Tam."

Mick puts the five foot tall prise bar back in its original position, starts to pull down on it and says,

"Right the two of you put your shoulder to that flap and open it!"

The three of them work on it at the same time with no immediate movement from it.

Mick pulls down on the prise bar again with all his strength and shouts into Terry's ear who is standing right next to him,

"Tel, you're going to prison if you don't move this <u>now</u>!"

Terry lets out a bear like growl that vibrates deep from inside his chest,

"Arrrrrrrrgh!"

The flap lets out a groan and starts to move slowly.

Mick shouts encouragement.

"Yes Big Man! Harder! Push!"

Terry's face contorts with effort.

"Yaaaaaargh!"

Mick manages to get the prise bar further under and get some purchase on it and the three of them manage to get it moving. Once they overcome the initial inertia, it lets out a loud metallic groan and starts to move faster and faster.

Once open, a load of muck and fat gives way and gets carried away with the flow of water.

Mick props the heavy steel flap open horizontally with the prise bar as the three of them breathe a sigh of relief and crouch down to look into the 9 foot tube.

The old sewer man points at the muck and 'fatbergs' now being washed away.

"There was our problem. Decades of silt, rusty hinges and fatbergs."

Tammar pulls the smartphone from the pocket of his rucksack. Not his one as that's with Christine. Everyone has left their phone with their wives or girlfriends. Sure enough the map facility shows that they are lined up with Skinner Place.

They take a few steps in together holding hands for balance. A tube train can be heard pulling into the platform underneath them.

Mick looks at Tammar concerned…

"Don't worry. It's sorted. It will be taken care of. At least we know we're in the right place."

A previous reconnaissance mission inside and outside the station shows that if they are lined up with a little cul-de-sac, Skinner Place, outside the back of the station then they are in the pipe above the platform and tracks at Sloane Square station.

At the far end of the 9 foot tube is another heavy steel flap, so effectively the tube above the station can be sealed off from the flow of water from either direction, most likely for maintenance work.

Terry wonders at the construction of the 9 foot tube and the way the heavy steel flap at either end seals it off. "Very nearly perfect!"

Tammar asks, "This is you Big Man. Good enough for what you need?"

"Yeah, should be fine. I need your…" He makes a circling gesture with his right index finger.

Tammar turns his back to Terry so that he may retrieve two small Ziploc bags from his rucksack.

"Small zipped pocket on my right. Careful with those Big Man, you know they're the most important things of the whole day."

Terry removes the two bags and for the time being tucks them into the top of his thigh waders.

"I know. I'll be careful" he says with a chuckle and a knowing grin.

Tammar sloshes through the water to the second steel flap to check up on a quiet Mick who seems to be loving his day's adventure.

"Ok Champ?"

A beaming Mick replies, "All good Son. This one opens away from us too, downstream as it was supposed to on the plans I saw for here."

As he walks back to the heavy steel flat they had trouble with to take something else out of his rucksack Tammar tells Mick and Terry, "I just need to go and spread the love."

Tammar returns from 'spreading the love' at the heavy steel flap and finds that Terry has already managed to get his rucksack suspended from the ceiling, dangling in the middle of the tube with the aid of thick plastic cable ties.

"How we doing Big Man?"

Terry returns an 'ok' gesture and a big, confident, excited, knowing smile from ear to ear.

"Oh yeah! It's going to be proper mental. I wish I could hang around to see it! What's the mobile phone signal like in here?"

Tammar double checks once more. "Three bars. All good."

Terry asks: "How's the old boy doing down there? I think he managed to move it a bit without the prise bar."

"Let me go and see." Tammar walks the remaining distance to Mick at the second steel flap. "How we doin'?"

"Yeah, jobs a good 'un. We can take out the bar from the upstream flap, close ourselves in and we've got no danger that we can't open this one. It's all good - trust me and then we just walk out of here.

"Ok. Come let's check with Big Man and get the bar and seal ourselves in."

Tammar offers a steadying hand to Mick who willingly accepts it. The two men's Wellington boots skid and slide a little as they walk back to Terry in the middle of the tube. He asks:

"Big Man are we all good to close up and exit downstream? It's going to work?"

"Yeah, we're all good here."

"You sure that the forensics won't be blown to shit with the explosion? This man has **got** to be framed."

Terry coolly replies, with a confidence in his professional abilities,

"Trust me, it's cool. Anything this side will be blown to shit. The cigarette ends and the corner from the magazine are going to make a miraculous survival for even the dumbest copper and forensics to find."

Tammar trusts Terry but can't help but make doubly certain, "Sure?"

Terry lets out a little chuckle, "Oh yeah, sure!"

Tammar says. "I know we're all wearing gloves and hairnets but no-one touch it. I don't want forensics picking up any clues."

Mick and Tammar very carefully, whilst holding hands, without touching it, squeeze past Terry's rucksack and make their way to the first heavy steel flap being held open by the prise bar.

Once past the rucksack Mick pauses and asks Terry,

"Detonators in yet?"

"No, not yet. Just waiting for you two to come back past it."

With his back to Tammar he mouths to Terry, "Watch this!" And gives Terry a wink.

Tammar asks Mick, "How do we get the bar back out? That thing weighed a ton! And took three of us to move it!"

The old pensioner walks up to the prise bar and grabs it with his right hand. He waits for the distinctive sound of a tube train entering the platform beneath them.

"One. Two. **Three!**"

In one swift simultaneous movement he delivers a quick back kick with the heel of his thigh waders to where the bar meets the floor. He's obviously done this before as you can tell he's hit the prise bar in the sweet spot so it slides out easily. He snatches the bar with his right hand so it is outside of the falling arc of the heavy steel flap. Then spins 45 degrees so he is facing Tammar, half way down on one knee like Al Jolson in the Jazz Singer pose, whilst wagging his left hand in a 'jazz hands' fashion. A thunderous metallic crash reverberates around the tube as the heavy steel flap slams shut behind him sealing them in.

Tammar crouches half way down as he puts his hands over his ears to protect them from the loud bang amplified through the tube. Terry can be heard cracking up with laughter at the prank the old boy has just pulled.

"Oh! The look on your face! Priceless!" Terry roars with laughter.

Tammar finds Mick's gag funny but can't help but worry that they are now trapped like rats in the 9 foot tube above Sloane Square station. He successfully manages to cover the slight tremble in his voice…

"I sure hope you're right as you said before "a hell of a job to try and move it from the other side". Now we're the other side and we had enough trouble trying to open it from the right side."

Mick flatly replies, "I hope so too!"

Mick and Tammar return back to Terry. Mick passes the prise bar to Terry and takes his hand to steady himself as his thigh wader boots skid a little on the fat and mud as he passes the rucksack.

Tammar takes Terry's hand to stop himself from skidding. As he passes the suspended rucksack he can see the two cigarette butts with Simon Rosenstein's DNA on them from the cab ride 6 months earlier. They have been carefully placed on a recessed part of the 9 foot tube, glued in with the aid of some tunnel fat. The corner that has been ripped out of the Robb Report magazine has been soaked in water and 'stuck' to the tunnel wall in the same way.

A minute later Terry completes his work.

Tammar asks, "All good Big Man?"

"Oh yes! Let's go."

Just as Mick promised, the second heavy steel flap opens much easier than the first and they are able to pass through and close it behind them, effectively making a closed container above Sloane Square station with Terry's rucksack suspended in the middle.

Looking back at the second flap, closed, over Sloane Square station.

They continue downstream for about another 30 minutes towards the Thames underneath Ranelagh Gardens.

Eventually they come to the large exit doors. On the other side will be the Thames and hopefully Roger.

Mick turns and asks, "How we doing for time Son?"

Tammar stops and pulls his sleeve back enough so he can read his watch.

"9.10am. We're late, very late. Because of the first flap being stuck. I also underestimated the difference in walking times between street level and walking carefully in this stuff. At street level from Cloacina to here took 25 minutes and 29 seconds. I allowed 40 minutes for walking plus 5 minutes for Terry's backpack. 45 minutes. It's taken us an hour and twenty five minutes. 40 minutes longer than expected. It's a good job the safes were open as we saved 10 minutes there but we're still 30 minutes down. I hope he's there ok."

Mick turns his back to the big exit doors and says,

"Now, when we come out the Thames can rise or fall by as much as five feet per hour and have a current of six knots. The tide is going to be higher than we expected as we're half hour late. Any later and we could have been in big trouble. Seeing as it's low tide now we should be ok but just respect it."

Terry voices his fears: "I hope the river police aren't waiting on the other side for us."

There is a silence for a moment. Tammar knows that if the river police are the other side of the doors then the game is well and truly up. They'd have nowhere to run to.

Mick aims to make Terry laugh and relax him a bit, "I know I'm too pretty for prison!" The old pensioner jokes.

Mick beckons to Terry for him to pass the 5 foot tall prise bar for the final time and the three of them lever open the Thames door to the welcome sight of daylight.

The three look up and down the Thames for a Police boat and armed officers with guns drawn standing on the banks but there is nothing. Just one blue, professional offshore racing powerboat waiting straight ahead in the middle of the Thames, bobbing gently with the current.

Mick turns on his fifteen million candlepower torch and waves the beam from side to side whilst Tammar waves his arms above his head. They manage to catch the attention of Roger who raises both arms in the air and impatiently taps at his wristwatch in frustration. He starts to manoeuvre the front of the boat in towards the outlet of the tunnel where the three men now walk down the slipway to the water.

The front of the boat points in to the step at the end of the slipway.

Tammar says "You first Mick. Take your time and do it right!"

Mick goes first and the ageing pensioner manages to successfully board with a helping hand from Roger and a shove from Tammar and Terry.

Next is Tammar who, once onboard, turns and helps Terry on. With all three successfully onboard Tammar excitedly shouts "Go! Go! Go!"

But instead of making their high speed escape on the fastest boat on the Thames, Roger simply starts to putter across the width of the river over to the south side of Chelsea Bridge where there are some steps leading up to Battersea Park.

Roger points to a small cool bag on the floor of the boat. "There's a cold bottle of water each there. You took your time! What the hell happened?"

Tammar passes a bottle each to Mick and Terry before taking a swig from the ice cold, half litre bottle of water but seems to have a little trouble swallowing.

"Ahh! Oh God that tastes good! We got stuck. One of the flaps above Sloane Square station was stuck fast. That and just the walking takes longer than you imagine. I timed it at street level and it took 25minutes and 29seconds. You do it down there and it just takes far longer than you would think."

Roger putters the power boat towards the steps up to Battersea Park. He's been kept in the dark for the past half hour and wants to know as much as possible.

"How about the job? Nothing's come over the radio or internet yet."

Tammar, now just relieved to be out from the tunnel breathing fresh air and looking at daylight answers,

"Cool like the Fonz. The safes weren't even closed let alone locked!"

Roger laughs, "You're pulling my plonker! Straight up?"

"Tell him Mick."

"Yep. We missed out on the fun of blowing them up."

The power boat nears the shore and Roger lines the front of the boat up as best he can with the steps up to Battersea Park at the side of Chelsea Bridge.

Tammar nodding at the park asks, "You sure you've thought out your exit strategy here?"

Mick smiles a broad, knowing smile.

"Oh yes Son! I've checked and there's no CCTV cameras on trees!"

Mick takes off the small, black Adidas backpack and passes it to Tammar,

"Thank you for including me today Son. I've had a blast. A blast! Get it?! Oh wasted I am, wasted here!"

Tammar chuckles at the old boy's joke,

"Nonsense. We couldn't have done it without you. I couldn't have done it without any of you. Thank you all very much."

In a very serious tone Roger says, "Send that slag down so he don't hurt anyone else."

Terry agrees, "Hear, hear!"

Mick steps forward and with a helping hand from Tammar and Terry he manages to jump out of the boat into the shallow water. The three watch as he wades up the shore and climbs the few steps to the fence and the park. He pulls out his bunch of six fire brigade keys and unlocks the padlock. After opening the gate and once safely inside, he locks the padlock, stands upright and looks to the boat. The old sailor salutes his three colleagues, takes his white hard hat off and bows for a job well done. As he walks off under the canopy of trees he starts to hum 'Crazy' by Patsy Cline. He keeps close to the foliage on the right hand side; with their green leaves they provide coverage from the steps down towards the car park just in case anyone should be watching from above in a helicopter.

After 150 metres he sits on a wall and strips off his thigh waders, body harness and white Microgard coverall to reveal a short sleeve light blue check shirt, a pair of dark blue shorts and thick boot socks. He carries the items at arm's length trying not to get any of the mud and muck over his fresh civvies. Another 60 metres further down sat on the grass on a rug with a picnic and reading a book is his 73-year-old 'dolly bird' wife, Jean. Their 14-year-old Nissan Micra car is parked a short distance behind her in the car park.

Jean puts a bookmark in place and looks up as she closes her novel.

"I watched you from here come out of the tunnel. You looked like a man half your age. I take it, it didn't all go quite to plan but someone looks happy. So a good day then love?"

Mick beams from ear to ear, very, very proud of his morning's accomplishments.

"All the better for seeing you my love. I enjoyed that picnic, shall we head off home?"

"Yes! Lets! I'll run us a nice bubbly bath. How about that?"

Mick pulls a soppy face which means 'I'm on a promise'.

Jean closes up the wicker picnic hamper and puts it on the back seat of the car after first opening the boot of the car to reveal it is lined with thick, clear, plastic sheeting. The white Microgard coverall, thigh waders, hard hat, head torch, hair net, body harness, red rubber gloves, latex gloves and thick boot socks are thrown in the boot of the car and quickly shut. Jean throws a pair of flip-flops by his feet and passes him a packet of baby wipes. Once he has wiped his hands and thrown the wipes into a carrier bag she holds for him, he holds out his hands so Jean can squirt hand sanitiser for him to rub all over his hands and wrists. They kiss and smile and rub noses like Eskimos before taking their seats in the little car. Slowly, with Jean at the wheel, they make their way out of the park and join the flow of traffic in Queenstown Road. Jean pushes a cassette into the car radio which plays 'their' song - Crazy by Patsy Cline.

Back on the power boat. Again, instead of roaring off at high speed with a devil-may-care attitude, Roger once more simply putters the power boat underneath Chelsea Bridge. Once they are underneath the bridge and out of sight, Tammar and Terry quickly take off their thigh waders and white Microgard coveralls down to their underpants. Roger has two fluorescent orange backpacks waiting, along with two pairs of fresh clean boots, baby wipes and hand sanitising gel.

Trying to look for something on the next bridge along Roger asks,
"Whereabouts is it Tam?"

Tammar pointing at the Grosvenor Railway Bridge a short distance down the river replies,

"Far side of the first arch from the right, on the right. I didn't want to make it too obvious for anyone watching from Chelsea Bridge to be able to see us."

Once Tammar and Terry are dressed in their new clothes Roger motors over to the Grosvenor Railway Bridge as trains pass overhead in both directions.

Inside the two backpacks all folded, were two pairs of orange hi-visibility t-shirts and orange railway workers trousers. Along with red and green hand flags for signalling trains and a blue enamel armband with white lettering saying 'COSS'.

Roger looks Tammar up and down from head to toe as he puts on the armband.

Tammar now has on a bright orange backpack, a bright orange t-shirt with reflective stripes, bright orange trousers, new black rubber soled boots, his white hard hat from before, blue enamel COSS armband and he rolls up the red and green hand flags for signalling trains.

"You sure you really need all that kit?"

"Easiest way to fool someone is to look the part, whatever that may be. It just so happens for the railway if I want to look the part of a P-Way man this is the kit that is expected to be seen."

"Fair enough. I hope you know what you're doing. That electricity up there is no joke. I knew a girl years ago when I was a kid. She climbed into a depot and got juiced up. The burns came out on her face. She must have tripped over while her foot was still in contact with the live rail. I don't know how she was so lucky. Seriously Tam that stuff up there will kill you stone dead. You remember Brian from Jarrow Road?"

"Yeah. The car guy. Used to restore the Triumph Stags."

"He was diagnosed with terminal cancer. He didn't want to wait for the end."

"And?"

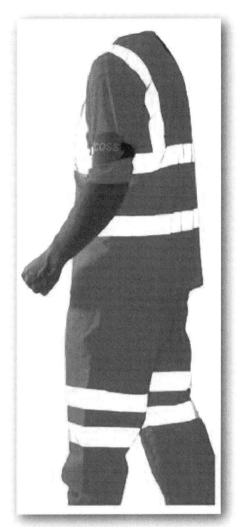

"And he rigged two jumper leads up to the mains so when he put it on he wouldn't be able to let go and electrocuted himself."

"Oh! Cheers mate! A comforting thought before we are about to go up to ten lines of trains and electric rails."

"Remember, it's not the voltage that kills you, it's the current!"

"What does that even mean?!"

"A taser gun will deliver 50,000 volts but won't kill you. Up there you'll have 660 volts and it'll fry you in an instant."

"Ok."

"Remember it's enough to push a train weighing hundreds of tons!"

"Yeah, I know mate. We'll try and be careful. Ok Roger, jokes aside, many, many thanks mate. You've really come through for us. You know where to meet Tizer yeah?"

"Yeah, no problem at all."

Tammar steps off the boat and onto a collapsible metal ladder with foot spacers, already in place from the night before to climb up onto the bridge. Terry waits to follow in case the thin, collapsible ladder won't take the weight of the two of them at the same time. Once Tammar has made it to the top he turns and waves down at Terry who bids Roger farewell and takes his turn. Once Terry has successfully made the climb and the two of them are safely on the bridge they unhook the ladder and let it fall into the deep of the Thames. They wave their thanks and goodbyes to Roger who *now* opens the boat up to make a quick getaway towards the sea without attracting too much attention to himself.

Tammar and Terry look at each other ..

Terry has to raise his voice to be heard over the noise from a train passing overhead.

"We've just taken all the risk and done all the hard work and he drives off with a backpack full of diamonds and jewellery. Can he be trusted Tam?"

"I think so."

Terry shrugs his shoulders and watches the boat go down the Thames toward Vauxhall Bridge.

Tammar says, "No one will dare cross Alfie if they like breathing. This project has become very personal for him. He views it as divine retribution for his Karen and that he is keeping other women safe. That's why all the contents from the safes were put into evidence bags and sealed up. If Roger thinks he's helping himself to a trinket on his run down the Thames then he's very much mistaken…Come on we best be quick."

The bridge thunders as two more trains pass overhead.

"The only way is up now. Nearly there. Come on."

Terry follows Tammar and the two men climb up inside the Grosvenor Railway Bridge. It's the bridge that all National Rail trains must cross over the Thames when they leave or enter Victoria station. They climb to just below track level and wait for another two trains to pass. Whilst they wait Terry asks, "What's the time?"

"9.28. The call will have been made. Send the text."

With that Terry pulls out a cheap, brand new, pay as you go mobile phone from his trouser pocket, sends one text and throws the mobile phone into the middle of the Thames.

Tammar follows suit and throws his smartphone into the middle of the Thames as they continue to wait for trains to pass.

Ever the knowledgeable cabbie Tammar looks up and down at the bridge: "Did you know that work on the original bridge was started in 1859 and had just two rail roads? In 1865 they widened it to increase the number of roads by a further five and then in 1901 they widened it again to add another two roads. The tenth road was added in the sixties when they rebuilt the whole bridge. In other words, watch yourself when we go up. If the electricity doesn't get you the trains will."

Terry looks around himself at the support structure of the bridge and says, "I'm surprised the Luftwaffe didn't try and take it out during World War 2. You take out the whole of Victoria Station if you take out this bridge."

"They did. They missed. Peabody Avenue over there on the right took the brunt of it." Pointing to his left Tammar continues,

"And over there, the Grosvenor canal used to stretch down as far as Terminus Place at the front of Victoria station. They used to have a canal in Victoria station so they could unload canal boats in the station. Mad isn't it?!"

There is silence from above as no trains can be heard coming or going. Tammar motions upwards with his head, "Come on quick! Now's our chance."

The two men, now looking like two railway track workers dressed in hi-visibility orange trousers and t-shirts, complete with hi-visibility orange backpacks, arm band, white hard hats and green and red flags, make the last climb up onto track level of the bridge where they come up by a signal gantry with a few coloured light signals on it. They gaze around at the view up and down the Thames on either side and the derelict Battersea Power Station behind them. On the side of the track is an insulated, super oversized spanner. Roughly 3 feet in length used for tightening the bolts on the sleepers.

"Tel, grab that big patrol spanner it'll help make you look the part."

Terry picks up the patrol spanner which when resting on its end on the ballast rocks of the track comes up to his hip.

A train approaches on the other side of the bridge going in towards Victoria and sounds its whistle. The two men raise their right arms and smile at the driver. As they have given the correct signal the train doesn't slow and continues over the bridge towards Victoria station.

Terry is anxious at how late they are running. They were supposed to be well gone by now.

"Time?"

Tammar checks his watch.

"9.31. Any second now."

Sure enough they start to see the headlights of the Gatwick Express train motoring towards them at line speed.

"Like clockwork."

"How fast is he going Tam?"

"I clocked it with Sat Nav and they're doing 30mph when they reach this point on the bridge."

"He is going to be able to see us and stop in time? He is your last chance, you know that don't you? You sure you know what you're doing?"

"Yep. We're in the perfect place. He'll be looking for this signal gantry when he leaves Victoria station. Just follow me and try and be silent and try not to look so big!"

The Gatwick Express train sounds its whistle and the two men raise both their arms above their heads in a 'don't shoot' type of pose.

The train whistles an acknowledgement before starting to slow.

Terry can't believe it, "Oh God it's actually working! He's gonna stop!"

"Shh! Just be cool. Act like you belong."

"Where'd you learn to do this?"

"Train drivers. I made sure I did some account work from the National Rail stations. Picked a few up, got them talking and they all agreed this was the way to do it."

The train slows. As the train nears them Tammar realises there is a fatal flaw in his plan which threatens to ruin everything.

"Oh crap!"

From the tone of Tammar's voice, Terry is instantly worrying.

"What's up? What's wrong?"

"There's no cab door on the train? How we supposed to get a lift?! Just act cool. Let me do the talking."

The train slows and stops perfectly alongside the two men.

The train driver gets up from his seat and walks across the cab. He lowers a side window and sticks his head out.

"Alright guys?"

As Tammar is wearing the Controller of Site Safety armband and the senior of the two he answers,

"Hello driver could we get a lift to Clapham Junction and Gatwick Airport for me please?"

"Yeah, no problem guys."

"I don't see a door though?"

"One moment I have a foot pedal here which will open just this passenger door behind me. Up you come."

Sure enough, a single passenger door behind the driver's cab opens up. Terry goes first sliding his super size patrol spanner onto the floor of the train and then grabbing the rails to help himself up into the train.

The train driver says, "That's a big one!"

Terry dryly replies, "I've got a big spanner too!"

Tammar gets into the train and the driver operates the foot pedal to close the door and the train pulls away.

Tammar whispers to Terry. "Thank God! I thought we were going to have to make small talk with the driver for the next half hour. No cab door I thought we were sunk! You know what to do at Clapham Junction?"

"Yeah, it's all cool. Isra is waiting for me at Dorking. I told her to wait not in the station car park as there will be CCTV but in one of the quiet side streets and to wait no matter how late I am. I took a tip from the Howard Marks book, 'Mr Nice' and made sure my final stop was not at my destination. Are you still good for time Tam? We were supposed to be on two trains before this one?"

"I don't know mate, I don't know. It's far too close for comfort. Six months worth of planning…"

Tammar is interrupted by the train driver shouting from the cab.

"Clapham Junction mate!"

Terry can't believe it. In only three minutes the train is at Clapham Junction station.

"That was quick! For a getaway vehicle - that's crazy! **Thank you driver!**"

Tammar is pleased at his choice of the quickest getaway car in London. "Yeah, let the train take the strain eh?!"

As the Gatwick 'Express' is supposed to be a non-stop service the train driver stops with just the front of the train at the start of the platform ramp. Just enough so Terry can get out of the first door at track level, taking his super size patrol spanner with him. Once on the track he takes a step back and gives a wave of thanks as the train pulls away, waits for 30 seconds and throws in disgust his patrol spanner back on the side of the track where it lands with a clank and thud. He tosses his hard hart down on top of the patrol spanner as he is finished with it.

He walks up the platform ramp and strips off his orange over trousers and t-shirt to reveal a pair of shorts and a simple sports t shirt.

He rolls up the fluorescent clothing, tucks them under his arm and does his best to mingle with the morning commuters and wait for the next train to take him to Dorking.

The Gatwick Express drives on, non-stop to Gatwick airport arriving at 10:02hrs.

Tammar steps onto the platform with the rest of the passengers and thanks the driver. He doesn't want to say anything too interesting or memorable or have the driver look at him and remember his face or really anything about him ten days from now. Just another P-way guy the driver gave a lift to. Tammar waits for the lift up to the airport and boards with eight other people. As the lift travels up Tammar once more looks around to make sure there are no CCTV cameras in the lift since his recent 'dry run'. He bends down as if he is doing his laces up when in fact he is actually untying both boots and making the laces as loose as possible.

When the lift reaches the top he lets the others out but he doesn't exit. Rather he has the empty lift back down to platform level to himself. He quickly steps out of the boots, pulls off his socks and strips off his orange safety trousers and t-shirt to reveal shorts and an Ultimate Fighting Championship t-shirt. From the back of his waistband he pulls a pair of flip-flops and throws them to the floor just in time as the lift door opens at platform level to reveal two police officers and a Springer Spaniel dog.

The officers stand to one side allowing Tammar to leave.

He instantly breaks into a cold sweat and thinks to himself "Holy crap!" He's got to think of something quick before they realise something is up.

"Forgot something. Got to go back." He says.

"Is that yours?" As they point at the pile of clothes and boots.

"No. Not mine."

"Best call that in."

Funnily enough the two policemen don't seem too concerned by it. They are busily engrossed in conversation and neither pays much attention to the Springer Spaniel sniffing the pile of clothing in the corner of the lift or Tammar until the lift nears the top when the first policeman says,

"He's interested in you."

Tammar's mind races. Surely the dog knows the orange clothes are his? What can the dog smell? The Westbourne? The C4 explosives? The hand sanitiser? Tammar's fear? He needs an instant funny comeback.

"Just as long as he doesn't sit down next to me eh?! The little grass! Company man is he eh?!" As he nods at the Springer Spaniel. "Member of the Federation is he?"

"No, the little scab! Aren't you Barrington?" Says one officer much to the annoyance of the dog handler.

Tammar and the police officer laugh before being joined by the second officer in laughter.

"Barrington?!" Says Tammar disbelievingly at the grandiose name for a dog.

The policeman rolls the pronunciation of the dog's full name in a thick Jamaican accent as it's only the three of them in the lift and there are no witnesses,

"*Mr Barrington Levy...* He *loves* the sensimilla! Don't you Barrington? His 'working' name is Barry."

The lift doors open and the officers and the dog go first.

"Come on 'Barry'. See you later. Have a good flight."

"Thank you." Says Tammar.

The two police officers and Mr Barrington Levy exit the lift. He appears to have gotten away with it. Trying to look cool and buy a bit of distance between himself and the police officers he deliberately starts patting all of his pockets in search of his train ticket to get through the barriers.

After finding his train ticket and passing through the ticket barriers to exit the train station he turns left and makes his way towards the south terminal heading for the Virgin Atlantic check in desks at the end in zone A.

He can't help but smile as sure enough Barrington Levy the little grass has sat down next to a young man who you would sum up as a marijuana smoker.

As he walks past he can just overhear the conversation between one of the officers and the young man. "When did you last smoke marijuana?"

He gets to the end of the south terminal where the Virgin Atlantic check in desks are as his son Liam spots him and runs to give him a big hug.

"Are we really going daddy? Are we really going? Mum said we might have to go back home if you couldn't make it!"

"Of course we're going son."

He looks up to see his long-term girlfriend, Christine and their daughter Daisy.

Mwah! He gives Christine a big kiss on the lips. She appears to have a little tear in the corner of her eye.

"Don't start that old pony" he jokily says to stop Christine from getting too emotional.

Holding back her tears of relief as best she can Christine says,

"You do like to cut it fine don't you?! Gonna give me a heart attack!"

Tammar leans forward and whispers in Christine's ear,

"It would all be good if it came on top. Journey times from place X to Gatwick you know what I'm saying. This way it looks impossible."

Christine dabs away at the corners of her eyes with a tissue.

"I was worried. I couldn't help it. Did it go ok?"

Tammar just nods and smiles. "I can still smell it in my nose. I've just met Barrington Levy in the lift!"

"Really?! The singer?"

"No! A police drug sniffer dog. He's just sat down next to some young guy down there."

Christine is still very concerned, choking back the tears she looks at the time.

"Come on we really must get you checked in. We've got less than 7 minutes left. We're all done. Here's your passport and your online check in thing."

As Tammar doesn't have any luggage he is able to use one of the check in kiosk machines.

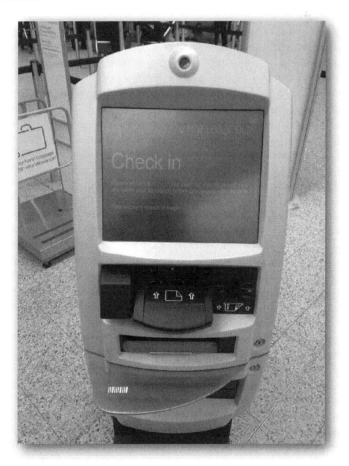

Tammar, Christine, Liam and Daisy head off to go through security quickly making their way down to gate 13 to start their holiday.

Chapter 8

Roger and Tizer

After dropping Mick off at Battersea Park and Tammar and Terry at the Grosvenor Railway Bridge, Roger races down the Thames to the Blackfriars Millennium Pier by Blackfriars Bridge on the north side of the Thames. As planned, despite it being low tide the pier is always afloat. Waiting amongst the tourists is a 5 foot 10 inch white male with close cropped ginger hair dressed in black shoes, black trousers, black shirt and a black tie with a single diamond earring in his left ear. Roger slows right down as the power-boat gently bumps against the rubber edge of the pier. Tizer steps forward and Roger says,

"You **must** be Tizer!"

Although he'd never met him you couldn't fake a head of ginger hair like that.

"Yes."

"These are for you then." He passes over the small black Adidas back-pack with the haul from the robbery along with Tammar's rucksack with the Dubarry Wexford Wellington boots inside. The bolt cutters and padlock have been thrown into the middle of the Thames on the run down here.

"There was a problem on the job. They couldn't get one of the flaps open. You know what to do with this lot?"

"Yes. Grandad told me what to do. Thank you. "

"Thank you. Good luck."

"You too."

With that Roger really opens up both engines and the true power of the offshore powerboat becomes evident. This display of power is a little too ostentatious for Tizer's liking who is surrounded by tourists waiting for the next tour boat to go down the Thames in either direction. He still has to get back up to street level before attention and eyes can be drawn to him and what has just gone on between the two of them.

Tizer quickly kneels down and puts the small black Adidas backpack into the bigger rucksack before putting that on using both straps knowing that his grandad would go absolutely berserk if the contents ended up at the bottom of the Thames.

The Blackfriars Millennium Pier has signs warning of the presence of CCTV but in reality there aren't any at all.

As he walks up the ramp of the pier back to street level of Victoria Embankment he pulls a black baseball cap out from inside his shirt and quickly puts it on pulling the peak down over his face. With CCTV coverage everywhere in the 'Square Mile', the one piece of advice he was given by his grandad was to "cover up that ginger nut!"

Once on the footpath at street level he walks quickly but not so quick to attract attention to himself as he makes his way along New Bridge Street. Tizer wants to escape from prying eyes as much as possible and has his route back to Hatton Garden all worked out and even timed out in advance. From New Bridge Street he takes a left into Bride Lane, Fleet Street, Poppins Court, St Bride Street, Shoe Lane, and St Andrew Street. He starts to feel a little more relaxed when he reaches the Prince Albert Equestrian statue at Holborn Circus as he is back where he works in Hatton Garden. Once there he pays visits to his grandad Alfie's three jewellery shops. At the first he is met by Nanny Shirley who takes him into the back room where the first evidence bag containing the loose polished diamonds is handed over. The two of them inspect the seal on the bag and they are both content that the bag has not been opened or tampered with in any way by Roger.

"Good work Tizer. You sure you weren't followed?"

"No Nan, I wasn't. I would have liked a motorbike to have met me though."

"Your grandad thinks no on this one. Give us a kiss and get going."

Tizer gives his grandmother a kiss on the cheek, leaves the store and walks further down Hatton Garden to his grandfather's second shop. Having three jeweller's shops in Hatton Garden helps to fence dodgy diamonds from all over the world. The London Underworld and those in the know, know that Alfie is your go to guy to fence stones if you are trusted enough to be a 'face' and get an introduction to him.

Tizer walks into the second shop and Karen is behind the counter serving a customer. The brother and sister catch each other's eye across the shop floor. Tizer quietly nods across the store to her and waits whilst she excuses herself from the customer and gets a second member of staff to take over. She gestures with her eyes for Tizer to follow her and buzzes him through to the rear of the shop.

Once out the back Karen and Tizer pull out the next evidence bag with the jewellery and watches in it. Once again the seal is inspected by the two of them. They both gasp at the contents of the bag all thrown in together. Gold and diamond encrusted Rolex watches, diamond earrings, bracelets, necklaces.

"Bloody hell Tizer!"

"I know!! Bloody hell! It all looks good stuff too! How much do you reckon?"

"Ph-eeew! I don't know. A lot! You best get going. Grandad will be waiting."

"Yeah. Ok Sissy. See you later."

Quietly Tizer leaves the shop, turns right and walks to the third and final jeweller's. As he enters the store grandad Alfie is waiting with his arms folded and a face like thunder. He exhales and gestures with his hands before tapping his gold Rolex President watch.

Before Tizer can utter a word of apology or explanation Alfie gestures to the back of the store.

Once out back he asks,

"What happened Tizer? Were you followed?"

"No Grandad."

"You sure?"

"Sure."

"**Sure?**"

"Yeah, I'm sure Grandad. Roger just seemed to reckon the job was running late. Something about a flap."

"Ok. What you got for me? Let's have the swag first."

Tizer pulls out the last of the evidence bags. This one is the least impressive looking to the untrained eye but has the highest value with the loose uncut diamonds and brick shaped packages containing more uncut diamonds with the accompanying Kimberley certificates.

Tut tut tut! "He's been a busy boy Tizer. Have you got his wellies?"

Tizer pulls out the two large evidence bags, each sealed and containing one of Simon Rosenstein's leather Dubarry Wexford Wellington boots now covered in Westbourne water and mud.

"Ok. Put them back in the rucksack. Go now and take them to this address."

Alfie starts to write out an address in Essex on a piece of Rizla cigarette paper and hands it to Tizer.

"Go on your motorbike to this address. Do you know where it is?"

I think so. I can always put it in the Sat Nav…"

Alfie abruptly interrupts him. "No Sat Nav. If you get stopped by the law eat the Rizla paper and remember the drill…"

Now Tizer interrupts,

"I know. I know. No comment. No comment. No comment. Not guilty."

Alfie continues, "If you should end up at a cop shop, call me and I'll send down Ralph to get you out. Now, when you get to this address, give Danny the Milk Tray Man the boots in the bags but keep the rucksack. Tell him they are from me and he will know exactly what that means. He will be waiting in for them. Don't enter his house. Don't take your gloves or helmet off. Give him the evidence bags with the Wellington boots in and thank him from me. Go to the yard and burn the rucksack, the balaclavas, the hairnets and everything in it. Wait until you've seen it all burnt to ashes. You understand me Tizer? Geezers' liberty is at stake here. Geezers who have helped our Karen today."

"I understand grandad."

"There's a good lad. Give us a hug and get going. Take the rest of the day off. Oh and keep the speed legal on the bike alright!"

The two exchange a man hug and Tizer pulls on a jacket, black motorcycle crash helmet and gloves and leaves the shop.

Whilst this has all been happening Roger on the powerboat has managed to pass under Tower Bridge, past the Millennium Dome and get through the Thames Barrier at Woolwich.

As the whole robbery is running late Roger's wife Janet is getting deeply engrossed in the love story she is reading on her e-reader whilst sitting in the driver's seat of their Land Rover Defender looking out to sea.

Janet loves a good bodice ripper novel, powerful male figures and forbidden love. So deeply engrossed in her novel does she become that she doesn't notice Roger's approach in the powerboat as her view has been partially blocked by the blind spot the snorkel of the Defender creates when looking out of the windscreen. She has failed to respond to Roger in their accustomed way of a triple flash of the headlights, which means, "I've seen you and I will back up the Land Rover and trailer into the sea."

This pleasant but low profile husband and wife team were in the past one of the most prolific drug runners on the south coast of England. They have long since retired from the drug running game. In the words of Roger, "Only a fool thinks he can get away with it forever." They quit while they were ahead. Tammar never knew of their 'sideline'.

Back when Roger was professionally racing the offshore powerboat everyone at the beach knew the husband and wife team of Roger and Janet.

They were always taking the powerboat in or out of the sea.

It was a familiar sight of this great big offshore powerboat on the back of its' trailer and the trailer hitched behind their Land Rover Defender.

The Defender would be breathing through its snorkel above the front windscreen whilst the sea lapped around the back of the vehicle.

Eventually no-one paid too much attention to this big powerboat going into the sea or coming back out - it was just Roger the powerboat racer. In fact no one paid any attention to the fact that Roger and the boat would be gone for hours at a time. Enough time to go over to the continent and back with contraband.

"Modern day prohibition" is what Roger called it. "History repeating!".

Back in the fantasy world of Janet's bodice ripper novel she was deeply enthralled by the dark languorous eyes of the lead character Clayton

Westmoreland, the Duke of Claymore and the heroine of the story, Whitney Stone, who had been bargained away by her bankrupt father.

Roger's wife Janet's fantasy world is disturbed by a mobile phone ringing and vibrating in the cup holder down to the side of her hip. She quickly looks up and now sees the powerboat waiting offshore. She looks back down to see on the screen of the brand new, cheap, pay-as-you-go mobile phone 'Big Daddy' calling.

"Sorry darling! I didn't see you. The snorkel was in the way! I'll back up now!"

Both Roger and Janet had been very media paranoid for many, many years and knew not to <u>ever</u> mention anything over a phone call, text or email that was of a sensitive nature.

By now Janet was excellent at backing the trailer into the sea and between the two of them they have the boat secured and are on their way in under ten minutes.

Once safely home Roger has been in the habit of always washing the interior of the boat down with a water and bleach solution. Today sees an improvement in his DNA cleaning of yesteryear. After the initial water and bleach wash he uses a well known household product with oxygen bleach for a second wash of the boat interior. DNA evidence destroyed. Bonfire lit. A well deserved sit down in the armchair with a cold can of Polish lager in front of the TV. Job done.

He toasts his absent comrades in arms,

"Good luck everyone!"

Chapter 9

Crime Doesn't Pay Someone Always Has To Go To Jail

W e see Tammar's eyes close up as if he is talking in the rear-view mirror of the cab & he speaks to us, the reader once again.

"They always say that doing something is the easy part but getting away with it is the hard part. Now, we all know that crime doesn't pay and that someone *always* has to go to prison. Right? **But,** did you know that there is, not a law in Great Britain, but more of a gentleman's agreement which says that before your film can get its age certification so it can be shown in the cinema it **has** to show that crime doesn't pay!

The Cinematograph Act of 1909 required that cinemas showing films to the public should be licensed by local councils to protect public safety.

The Act said nothing about censorship or about the content of films shown. However, local authorities soon began imposing their own conditions in the licences they issued to cinemas, including restrictions on the showing of films of an 'objectionable character'.

The chaos caused by these very vague and often varying from council to council, licensing tests, led directly to the formation of the BBFC, the British Board of Film Classification, in order to impose some kind of consistency on the films being shown.

Because the police had expressed some concern about films inciting young people to commit crime, when the BBFC started work in 1913 it said it would not approve any 'scenes calculated to act as an incentive to crime'. Nonetheless, it took some time before councils around the country would accept the BBFC's classifications. This was not in full until the 1920's when London recognised the BBFC and there was still a lot of variation in licences, leaving cinemas in many areas still vulnerable to charges. Therefore, in 1916 the Home Office issued model licensing conditions showing local councils what kinds of conditions they felt should be imposed. The 1916 model licensing conditions stated that films should not be exhibited, whether passed by the BBFC or not, that 'would be likely to encourage or incite to crime or lead to disorder'.

These were only model conditions, rather than something legally imposed, but in practice most councils began including such conditions in their licences. Those conditions, in effect, therefore gained legal force, although they did not originate in a piece of legislation, because they were part of the conditions of licenses that were being issued under the 1909 Act.

Think about it. All your life, have you ever seen a film where the baddies got away with it? No, never. The original Italian Job, they're in the coach with the bullion stuck on the edge of the cliff. They **never** get away with the proceeds do they? And we're no different. Someone has got to go to prison right? It's the rules. It just turns out that that person is not going to be me."

We now look across to a beautiful diamond ring on Christine's finger that sparkles in the bright sunshine and looking up at her face we see that she is wearing a white Minnie Mouse ears bridal hat.

We now look back at Tammar who looks a little awkward wearing a black Mickey Mouse ears groom's hat.

We look next at their son Liam who is wearing a Disney 'Pirates of the Caribbean' costume looking very happy waiting for the 3pm parade to start near Cinderella's castle in The Magic Kingdom theme park in Walt Disney World, Florida. We look next at Tammar & Christine's daughter Daisy who is wearing a Disney princess outfit but as we look up we notice she is bald, pale and thin.

Tammar turns to Daisy and says, "I told you I'd do it princess! I told you I'd keep my promise and you'd get your wish for us all to come out here and I'd marry mummy!"

Tammar turns to talk to us the reader once again, "Back in the day the police used to 'verbal' people. Saying they said something under interview which they later denied, to help secure a conviction. So now interviews are recorded. Now you have forensics which are 'irrefutable' so the police tamper with evidence to secure a conviction. To be honest I don't entirely blame them. What would you do to secure a conviction? You know he's guilty right? But the rules are stacked against you. The criminal breaks all the rules but gets upset when the policeman doesn't follow all the rules. I guess that's human nature. The Great Train Robbers were framed. The yellow paint on the foot pedal of the clutch of one of the jeeps used in the raid which later turned out to be the depth of a stroke from a brush but no paint on the carpet where you would rest your foot after changing gear & then on the sole of Gordon Goody's shoe. He admits he was a Great Train robber but says that evidence against him was fabricated.

Bill Bowl, a friend of Roger Cordrey, another one of the robbers, was an innocent man who went to prison for the robbery because the police planted evidence to frame him. The same yellow paint on a brass watch winder found in the lining of his coat. Sentenced to 24 years & died after 7 years in prison.

So what we did was to use forensics to our advantage and frame Simon Rosenstein with multiple 'evidences' so even his own solicitor will tell him "go guilty". What doesn't speak doesn't lie.

Remember back in the winter when Alfie asked if there would be enough time and I replied… "That I don't know. Maybe a prayer to the man upstairs on that one." and "Six months, fingers crossed. I've got to research some stuff and pull it all together but I'm thinking six months."

Well, I had to research it, figure it all out, try and put the team together, make all the pieces of the puzzle come together and then wait for tide heights on the Thames and flights out to Orlando from Gatwick airport. We needed a Monday so there would be ambiguity about when the raid had been carried out and also flights out to Orlando. We needed to fly from Gatwick because of where we would come out and this way it looks impossible should we be suspected, as to how you would get from Knightsbridge or central London to Gatwick airport in under 30 minutes. The only place that is possible is from Victoria station and with all the CCTV in the world in Victoria station not one camera would show us there as, well, we quite simply weren't there. We also needed low tide on a Monday because as Mick pointed out the Thames can rise or fall by five feet per hour. Where the Westbourne comes out into the Thames is under water most of the day. So our exit was limited and only possible at certain times and on certain days to make it all fit together like the gears of a clock. You understand what I mean?

Daisy, as you might have guessed is terminally ill. She has Neuroblastoma which is a rare childhood cancer of the nervous system.

Initially she was complaining about pains in her stomach and legs. We took her to the GP and A&E several times and after a CT scan it showed she had a large tumour in her abdomen. Unfortunately our little princess was diagnosed with Stage 4 high risk Metastatic Neuroblastoma which means the cancer had spread to her bone marrow and was prevalent throughout her skeleton, particularly in her legs, spine, skull and chest.

Neuroblastoma is a rare form of childhood cancer. Only one hundred children a year in the UK are diagnosed with it. Of those one hundred nearly half will be like Daisy's and have the life threatening Stage 4. Neuroblastoma is second only to domestic incidents in the cause of childhood fatalities in the UK.

Back in the winter she was given a slim chance of survival. On her little bucket list was 1) For me and her mum to get married, 2) For her to be the bridesmaid, 3) To come to Walt Disney World in Florida and 4) To be a Princess for the day.

As you can imagine both getting married and a family holiday to Florida are expensive on a single income. Well, then I had Simon Rosenstein in the back of the cab and it all fell into place. He was bragging about the value of the diamonds in his shop, the smuggling and the girl he had just attacked. The penny dropped pretty quick about who it was he attacked and where. I knew it had to be Alfie's granddaughter Karen that he was talking about. The idea about the river came to me because of the route we took down from Lowndes Square. The guys involved in the job quickly came to mind and as luck should have it for one reason or another, each would be sympathetic to my cause."

In the offices of the Make-a-Wish Foundation a letter is being opened and a cheque being pulled out for £15,850,000 from a Mr Alfie Walker. The trade value of the total proceeds of the robbery.

Tammar continues, "You see everyone on the robbery worked for free. No-one took a penny. OK, I palmed one of the stones and we've had it put into a ring setting over here. That was why I had trouble swallowing that mouthful of water on Roger's boat. 'Uncle' Alfie & 'Auntie' Shirley paid for our wedding and family holiday out here as a thank you for finding the man who hurt their Karen, which was very, very kind of them. Alfie & Shirley love Make-a-Wish because of their deceased granddaughter. Mick & Jean never could have kids and to be able to send terminally ill kids over here to grant their dying wishes appealed to them. Terry had a sister who died when he was six and she was four. Roger's wife Janet was raped before they got together and he has seen the damage it has done to her, so he was sympathetic. And Tizer, he's a good lad; he just knew to do what his grandad told him. Danny or the Milk Tray man as we call him, I've never met but Alfie tells me he owed him a favour and he came through for us, bang on."

"Now. So we've proven that crime doesn't pay but I also said someone always ends up going to prison but that person just wasn't going to be me. Don't worry all of the team got home safely and no-one has been in any trouble with the police whatsoever because as far as the police are concerned they have their man bang to rights."

"Do you remember Terry sent a text message when we were waiting on the Grosvenor Railway Bridge before we threw those two pay as you go mobile phones in the river? That was a text message to remotely detonate the suspended rucksack hanging in the tube above the platforms at Sloane Square station.

A bomb scare had been phoned in just before 9am to make sure it was all cleared out and trains were suspended in both directions. The explosives were remotely detonated by text message to a mobile phone detonator like the Madrid metro bombs, which incidentally were before 7/7 in England, why on earth you'd want to blow yourself up I don't know?

Anyway, 09:28hrs the tube above the tracks at Sloane Square station goes boom! If it went as we planned then there should be a great big hole pouring water onto the tracks. The police are going to investigate this 'act of terrorism' and go into the tunnel where they will find "the most important thing of the day". Remember me saying that? Well, the most important thing of the day was the evidence we were going to plant at the scene of the explosion. Remember I had Simon Rosenstein in the back of the cab and he smoked those two cigarettes and I said I was going to bite my tongue on that one? That's because there was a plan forming in my mind. I put on the latex gloves and with the tweezers picked up the two butts and put them in the Ziploc bag? The only conversation I started up with him was about the Robb Report magazine and overhearing he was going to the airport later that evening I arranged to collect him from his house. I brought him my two brand new copies of November & December's Robb Report magazines, which I hadn't read or even taken out of the plastic yet hence no finger prints except his.

After I'd dropped him off at Heathrow airport I put on a pair of latex gloves, always good to have a pair of latex gloves with you just in case - you never know. I selected page 259 of December 2012's Robb Report magazine and ripped a generous portion of the corner out. It has three photos of the interior of a Maserati GranTurismo Sport similar to Simon Rosenstein's new toy that he was admiring earlier that day. Plus it's a big enough clue that when the police were eventually going to search his house, as they are bound to, they are going to be looking for a copy of December 2012's Robb Report magazine because they are kind enough to put the date and the name of the magazine at the bottom of each page. Thanks to the Milk Tray man the two magazines are now back in his house in Chigwell along with the Dubarry Wexford Wellington boots. The Maserati corner of the magazine will hopefully be enough of a nudge to get the police to take a look inside the car where they will find, like the Great Train Robbers, muck from inside the Westbourne where your foot would rest if the Maserati had a clutch pedal.

Take a guess what evidence the police found inside the bombed out tunnel above Sloane Square station? - That's right, 2 cigarette butts with Simon Rosenstein's DNA on them and the corresponding missing corner to a magazine in his house.

Before the robbery we got the Milk Tray man to sneak into Simon Rosenstein's house, take his two Dubarry Wellington boots, and put them in the soil in his garden. We took a gamble that soil from Chigwell would be identifiable to the area and that's why I wiped the sole of his £350 Dubarry Wellington boot on the manhole cover in Hyde Park by the Serpentine as we went in for the first time. We also got the Milk Tray man to take Terry's brand new rucksack and put it on the soil in Chigwell in the hope that Chigwell soil would be discovered on scraps of rucksack after the explosion. I got the idea for the Chigwell soil from the Audrey Hepburn film 'How to Steal a Million'. In the film her dad is forging a painting by Vincent van Gogh; to the finished painting he adds dirt from the neighbourhood of Van Gogh. A nice touch no? We got the Milk Tray man to get us some soil from Simon Rosenstein's garden.

Remember I soaked the two boots in the Westbourne before making the footprints in the basement of his shop? Yes, they would find the prints of 3 pairs of Century 4000 thigh waders and the print of the Dubarry Wexford.

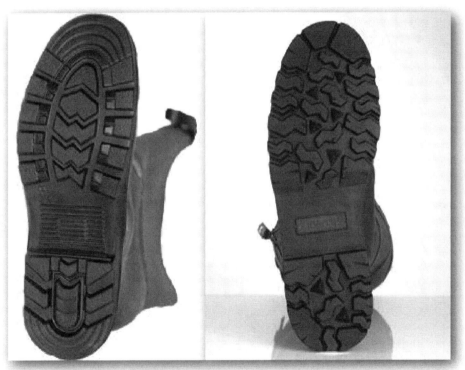

Century 4000 on left   Dubarry Wexford on right

And as a bonus on top of it, which was more than we could have hoped for, was the fact that he left the safes open. Not because we didn't have to blow them up to get into them but the fact that small particles from the explosion of the sewer wall from us getting in were found inside the safes. To the police's way of thinking, you were in on it.

The damning evidence against Simon Rosenstein in the end was:

1) Chigwell soil on manhole flap at the Dell.
2) Dubarry boot print in basement of shop. Unique wear to sole of boot provides unique wear print and can be matched up by the police.
3) The two safes were already open.
4) Particles from explosion into basement were found by forensics <u>inside</u> the two safes.
5) Corner of page 259 of December 2012's Robb Report magazine was found in the tunnel above Sloane Square station.
6) Corresponding magazine with only his finger prints on and missing the exact corner found at his house.
7) Chigwell soil on rucksack scraps found above Sloane Square station.
8) Westbourne mud in Maserati on footrest.
9) And the daddy of all evidence- the 2 cigarette butts with his DNA on them, found in the nine foot pipe over Sloane Square station.

You can't fake evidence like that. You're going down with that evidence and so he shall. At the moment he's in trouble and it's only going to get far, far worse for him.

Guess where he ended up? Parkhurst? Not quite but Alfie did have a reception committee at the prison he ended up at to make sure he got a very warm welcome. Yes, very warm indeed. Boiling sugar water in his boat. In prison terms that's known as 'napalming'. If he'd have gone in as a rapist he might have ended up in segregation but this way he's ended up in general population and Alfie gets the pound of flesh he wanted all along. It was a win, win, win situation. It was a shame that Karen was attacked but he won't be hurting anyone else anymore. He won't be inflicting his nastiness on anyone - we've made sure of that.

The actual blowing up of the pipe really will make no sense and it will be interesting to see what the media and police make of it. The smart amongst them might even suspect that he is being framed but the evidence will be irrefutable. '**What doesn't speak doesn't lie**'. He'll go down for a long time protesting his innocence and that is what we want."

Tammar turns to his Daisy and starts to sing,

"When you wish upon a star, makes no difference who you are. Anything your heart desires will come to you…"

We now leave a happy Tammar, Christine, Liam & Daisy with Cinderella's castle in the background, at Disney's Magic Kingdom theme park at Walt Disney World in Florida to enjoy their holiday as the music for the 'Celebrate A Dream Come True Parade' starts. How appropriate!

Printed in Great Britain
by Amazon